The Music Box

Books by T. Davis Bunn

The Quilt
The Gift
The Messenger
The Music Box

The Maestro
The Presence
Promises to Keep
*Return to Harmony**
Riders of the Pale Horse

The Priceless Collection

Secret Treasures of Eastern Europe

1. *Florian's Gate*
2. *The Amber Room*
3. *Winter Palace*

Rendezvous With Destiny

1. *Rhineland Inheritance*
2. *Gibraltar Passage*
3. *Sahara Crosswind*
4. *Berlin Encounter*
5. *Istanbul Express*

*with Janette Oke

T. DAVIS BUNN

The Music Box

BETHANY HOUSE PUBLISHERS
MINNEAPOLIS, MINNESOTA 55438

The Music Box

Inside illustrations by Lorraine Andrews Major.

Unless otherwise identified Scripture quotations are from the King James Version of the Bible.

Published by Bethany House Publishers
A Ministry of Bethany Fellowship, Inc.
11300 Hampshire Avenue South
Minneapolis, Minnesota 55438

Printed in the United States of America.

ISBN 1-55661-900-6

This book is dedicated to

TERRY & MARILYN

friends beyond distance and time

and

HAYES

whom I dearly hope will become a friend someday

and, most especially,

JACK

my new godson
with love

You have turned on my light!
The Lord my God
has made my darkness
turn to light.

Psalm 18:28, TLB

By the age of thirty-one, Angie Picard felt as though she had lived enough for seven lifetimes.

She paused in the front foyer of her little house and inspected her reflection. A nice oval face stared back at her, with light blue eyes and unlined brow and a brief afterthought of a nose. As she pinned her blue hat into place, Angie wondered again how all that had happened seemed not to show.

She had a habit she practiced each morning, a way of putting aside her inside thoughts and preparing for the day. As usual, she paused before opening the door and looked down at the antique crystal bowl, the one she left on the entrance-hall stand. She never opened that container, nor had she lifted the beautifully etched lid with its ornate silver filigree in years. She did not even touch it, except to give it a quick wipe with the dusting cloth once a week. Yet as she stood there, Angie mentally placed inside the crystal bowl everything she did not wish to take outside with her.

The aged doorframe was out of kilter, and she had to slam the door hard. Paint fell like a scattering of dirty snow from the porch roof. The house was old and in need of more care than she could give it.

Angie locked her door, then turned and took a grand breath, trying to draw in all the world and all the freshness of new beginnings.

Her porch was just big enough for two rockers, a swing, and peeling banisters laced with climbing roses older than she was. Angie stepped to the edge and peered at the sky, as if checking the weather, in case anyone was watching. But in truth she was making sure all the inside thoughts were carefully put away. Satisfied, she started down the walk to the street. For the moment, all was as it should be.

Despite her strongest efforts and her most fervent prayers, though, the thoughts had a way of escaping all on their own. Each evening when she returned from school, they were there, lurking in the shadows of her empty parlor, waiting for her to unlock the door and walk in and join them. Angie had often wondered, if she sold the house would the thoughts be able to follow her? But she was not likely to sell it. With her parents retired down to the coast, the little house often seemed like the only family she had.

Angie always gave herself plenty of time for the walk to school. On cloudy days such as this, the surrounding foothills were mist covered and mysterious. Somehow their green depths seemed nearer, as though in the night they had moved up close to her small town for comfort. She turned onto the street and walked briskly along, breathing in the fresh autumn air.

October was generally a grand month, and this

one was no exception. The mountains held in the night's chill, and days were generally fifteen degrees cooler than in the big flatland cities farther east. Nights were close enough to frosty that the trees began hearing the first knells of coming winter. They shivered in the slightest breeze and bent sorrowfully over summer's passage in the misty rains. They began drawing their autumn cloaks about them, congregating in russet flocks upon the hills, dressed in colors so subtle they were best seen on low-light days like this. The smell was sweet and close, and the incense of nature's cathedral filled Angie's nostrils as she walked.

The century's second great war was only six years gone, and already there were rumblings of another. The radio and the city papers were full of talk about places like Korea and Russia and provinces in China. These were worrisome times, at least down below in the cities where the world seemed eager to crowd in and take over.

Up here in their narrow mountain valley, the passage of seasons had a way of moving with caution. Folks showed their stubborn streak and dragged their heels at the rush of time. Too much was being cast aside without a backward glance. Too many good things lost in the swirl of events. The world raced on toward an uncertain future, and most people in Angie's hometown grew ever more grateful for the life they lived and loved and were determined to protect.

Almost every car that passed honked or gave

her a friendly wave. No one stopped, however, not any longer. Her quiet walks to and from school were well known and respected. Most of these hard-working families would never have dreamed of going anywhere without the car for company, unless it was a Sunday or a special occasion like a picnic; still, Angie's ways were a part of her, like the little hats she wore throughout the cooler months. Country people had a way of accepting such habits from one of their own.

Today, however, a car pulled over in front of her and a lace-gloved hand emerged through the passenger window to wave with frantic little motions. Angie prepared her smile as she approached and lowered her head to look inside the huge Plymouth. "Morning, Emma. Hello, Luke."

"Miss Angie." Luke Drummond was a big raw-boned man who ran the local hardware store. He measured out his words with the same caution as he did his wares. He tipped a sweat-stained hat to her, then went back to peering through the windshield—his way of granting the ladies privacy.

"Now, Angie, just look at your shoes. You've got them all wet with dew, they'll stain right through." Emma's voice through the passenger-side window was brisk.

"I do not care to shape my habits around the needs of shoe leather," Angie replied archly. "And besides, I've got my walking shoes on and my dress ones in here." She raised a small canvas bag for inspection.

"If you say so." Emma Drummond was her oldest and best friend, a heavyset woman who taught music class in the morning before helping her husband with their store in the afternoons. She also led the church choir, a sticking point between them. "What's that on your shoulders?" she wondered, shaking her head.

"Paint," Angie replied, brushing impatiently.

"Looks like a terminal case of dandruff. If I've told you once, I've told you a thousand times, you need to see to your house before it falls down around your ears."

Emma was a dear friend, but she had a way of trying to run everybody's life. "It's almost more than I can manage, seeing to the rooms I use," Angie sighed. "The exterior is just going to have to take care of itself. Besides, it's done all right through more years than either of us have seen."

"Humph." Clearly unconvinced, Emma peered at her friend. "What's got you dressed so somber? You look like you're headed to a funeral, not to school."

The sunless morning seemed to take on a more bitter chill. Angie reminded her friend with a question of her own, "Are you still going to the city this afternoon?"

"It's Wednesday, isn't it?" Then Emma remembered and momentarily faltered. "Oh, dear. I clean forgot. Seems like the years spin by faster and faster."

"Three o'clock, please. I have to be down there

on time. Now if you'll excuse me, I can't be late for school." She moved on down the sidewalk.

"Then you ought to let us drive you the rest of the way," Emma called out.

"If I did not have my walk and my morning quiet time," Angie replied as the heavy car scrunched up to cruise alongside her, "I positively do not know how I would manage to survive the day."

"Then we'll leave you be," Luke said, which stifled any further comment from his wife. "I'll make sure Emma is there on time, Miss Angie."

"And a good day to you as well, Luke." She watched the car drive off and reflected that Emma was much like a kite in a strong wind. It was only Luke's steady hand that kept her from flying off to goodness knows where. As it was, the two of them fit together as well as a hand inside a tailored glove. The vast majority of their customers chose to come in the afternoons; Luke saw to their orders while Emma fed them with news and lore and friendly visiting. Angie sighed again and firmly pushed away thoughts of all that was to come that afternoon. It would be good to travel down with Emma. Her friend's lively chatter would help fill the empty spaces.

Angie Picard climbed the great stone steps to the town's school, reflecting how going to the city was always referred to as "down," although the city was built on a series of hills and in parts was higher than their little valley. But that was just the geography and social studies teacher in her doing the talking.

The school was far too grand for their town. But the valley had been declared a county seat back before the hills had proved to hold no mineral richer than good topsoil. The town had used its first flush of state money to build a courthouse and county hall and school; the red-brick exteriors were dressed with stately Doric columns. Beyond the school fields, a deep-flowing river cut a musical swathe through the town's center. More state money had been used to erect a series of fanciful bridges, all stone and wrought iron. Over time, the town's burgeoning population had done its best to continue the fashion, so that most of Main Street was done up in stone and brick and handwrought balustrades. The result was a charming place in which even the most taciturn of hillfolk took pride.

The first bell of the day sounded just as she was slipping from her walking shoes into her pumps, which Angie took as a signal that the clock was running correctly. Habits and timing helped to frame her life, and they kept things like emotions in their proper place.

Angie greeted the other incoming teachers and walked the swiftly crowding halls to the library. She responded to "Hi, Miss Picard" tossed her way with a nod and a small smile. She was known not to speak at such times. The students had long since accepted that one of their favorite teachers kept herself aloof and isolated outside the classroom.

The librarian's silent habitat gave her no more use for empty words than Angie. They exchanged nods as Angie made her way over to the school's meager supply of record albums. She pulled out the album she sought, knowing the tattered cover so well she no longer needed to read the script. Another nod, then out the doors and down to class.

Already the tension was building, an electric thrill that kept her going through all the year. She lived for this. Teaching was what defined her life. Watching the excitement of discovery light up a young face was a joy so powerful she often needed to turn away toward the blackboard until she could regain her composure.

Her eighth-grade classes proceeded in orderly fashion, this day's lecture marked by periods of music. Angie used the music to help them picture the era as she described the courts of Europe and the politics and the fashions. She also used maps and reproductions and paintings, adding to the collage upon her walls until by the end of term there was scarcely a free space to be found.

The surprise came in the last session, when the day was wearing down. Angie was finding it increasingly hard to hold on to her enthusiasm, both because she was tired and because of what the day still held. She almost missed it, having played the music four times already, and her attention was distracted by the coming trip to the city. But she happened to look up a moment sooner than usual.

She often looked down or away when music

was playing, so the students did not need to concern themselves with how she saw them, and hopefully they could lose themselves in the music. But this afternoon, growing impatient to have the musical interlude and the class and the schooltime over with, Angie glanced at the wall clock and then at the students, and saw her.

The girl sat as always in the back row. Melissa Nealey was a little thing, so undersized Angie had checked the records to make sure she was not in the wrong class. She was also a newcomer, which in a hilltown meant she was too much alone. But Melissa was so quiet and so shy that the isolation seemed to suit her. Angie had tried on several occasions to draw her out, but the child had replied with monosyllables, clearly anxious to be away. There were none of the warning signs Angie had come to recognize—Melissa's test scores were good, her clothes were always clean and pressed, her hair combed and her eyes clear. And shyness was not necessarily a bad thing, especially in a newcomer.

But when Angie looked up, she saw that the little girl was turned toward the window, tears streaming down her face.

Angie lifted the needle from the phonograph record and said with forced brightness, "Now, who can tell me what that melody was?"

She waited a moment, then continued, "How about someone in the back?" She noted the quick little movement of a hand to wipe cheeks dry, then said, "Melissa, yes, we haven't heard from you today. Do you know the name of that lovely piece?"

A very quiet voice replied, "Greensleeves."

"Excellent." Angie wanted to keep the others from glancing around, so she unrolled a poster and tacked it to the cork panel behind her desk. "What can you tell us about this music?"

"It's a … a love song," she said softly. The voice was barely above a whisper and was spoken toward the window. "Two people have to say good-bye, but they don't want to."

"Very good," Angie said, tapping the poster with her pen.

As she launched into her summary of what life was like in sixteenth-century England, and what role the church played, and how radical such folk songs were for that time, Angie could not help but wonder at how the girl's words had tugged at her own heart.

Thankfully, the bell sounded on time. Angie waited until most of the class had filed out before calling Melissa over. The youngster had recovered her composure and had retreated back behind the quiet mask she usually wore. Angie looked into her eyes and started to ask if anything was the matter, when it hit her with the force of a silent thunderbolt: Despite their difference in age, Angie felt as though she were looking into a mirror. The thought held no logic, but the force kept her silent a moment longer, sitting there behind her desk, staring at the quiet little form in front of her.

Finally Angie cleared her throat and simply

said, "You certainly do know your music, Melissa."

For some reason, the words brought more tears welling to the young girl's eyes. But she bit her lip and held on to control. "I have to go," she said eventually. "My daddy is waiting for me."

Angie nodded her dismissal and waited until Melissa was at the door before saying, "If there is anything bothering you, Melissa, you may always come and speak with me. Anytime."

Melissa gave the scarcest of nods before vanishing through the open door.

"You'd think she was closer to nine than thirteen, she's so small," Angie said to Emma on the way out of town. "I spoke to a couple of the other teachers. They haven't had two full sentences from her in the month she's been here."

"I have her in my choir class." Emma nodded her agreement. "Tried twice to get her transferred. But the principal in all his glorious wisdom points to this note on Melissa's permanent record."

"What note is that?"

"Something from her school down in the city. It says she has one voice in a million, that's exactly how it reads."

"But she won't sing?"

"Not a peep."

Angie started to remark on the girl's strangeness, but at that moment they passed by the town bridal shop. A grand sign above the display read, "Everything for your perfect day!" Angie suddenly found herself awash in memories, ones she normally did not allow to accompany her beyond her own front door. But today was different, and the past rushed in through the open car window.

As the safety of their little town was left behind,

Angie reflected on the mistakes that had brought her to this place. And they truly were mistakes. She could not deny the fact, not here, not now.

She had first left this town to attend the university and become a teacher. Her problem was, she had left more than home behind. Her faith, for example. And the habits that had ruled her early life. All had been set aside in the city, where she had known no one and could lose herself in all the cold pleasures.

There in the city she had met Stefan. Bold, loud, dashing, and charming. And foreign. Stefan had been everything that she was not. His family ran the town's biggest and best Greek restaurant. He had a problem with his feet, something serious enough to keep him out of the army, yet not enough to hamper either his looks or his smooth way on the dance floor. And he had, quite literally, swept this mountain girl right off her feet.

His family had been opposed to the quiet-spoken girl from the beginning. Which was one reason why Stefan had taken to her so swift and strong. He was destined to enter the family business, so tied by blood and obligations that there was little room for even dreaming of another destiny. So he had rebelled as much as he dared and brought an outsider into their closed ranks.

She truly had loved her dashing Greek. So much so that she had been willing to cast aside her dreams of becoming a teacher and accept the role of waitress in the Greek restaurant, beneath the glowering disapproval of Stefan's mother. And father. And uncle and aunt and three cousins and four others whose connections were so flimsy that she had never managed to get them straight. The only one who had granted her an open-hearted welcome was his sister, Gina, the same lively woman who had invited Angie to attend church with her. Soon after their wedding, Gina had also brought Angie to the church's Bible study and thus helped her retrace her steps back to faith.

The wedding itself had been the noisiest affair Angie had ever attended, with singing and dancing and toasts and crashing plates and more dancing and more toasts. For a brief moment, Angie had managed to believe that all the family recriminations and arguments that had marred their courtship were behind them. But instead, they had simply been set aside for a single noisy night. The men had danced linked by handkerchiefs, Stefan dragged up time after time until he had collapsed gripping his chest, the first indication anyone had of his weak heart. But that night no one had paid any mind, just laughing and pointing and putting it down to a bridegroom's nerves.

There were memories of other noisy days as well, rising unbidden to fill her mind as she had watched the road broaden and take them farther into the lowlands. Days spent in the sweltering heat of the restaurant kitchen, rushing in and out, her customers' orders going unheeded, as no one could catch her quiet tone over the tumult. Feeling the mother's sullen eyes follow her everywhere. Trying hard to please, and knowing that nothing would break down the hostile walls—nothing except a baby.

Everything would be fine, Stefan had assured her over and over, just as soon as they had their first child. Then she would be accepted as one of the family. How could they reject the mother of one of their own? It was impossible. She would automatically become a part of them, connected by bonds of flesh and blood. She had no reason to worry, Stefan had said. Their first baby would make everything right, and every child after that would only make things better.

Eleven had been the telling number of their relationship. Eleven giddy weeks of courtship, just long enough to finish the university term. Angie had held on to that, though she was giving up graduating in order to join Stefan in the family business. Eleven months of trying to make the marriage work, gradually building up her courage to tell him that it was impossible—she could not bear to spend the rest of her life in a job she hated, under the eye of people who hated her, so she was going back to finish her degree. And then on the last day of the eleventh month, receiving the news that had shattered her life yet again. And ended her marriage as finally as the waiting grave. She would never have a baby, the doctor had told her. The tests were conclusive. It was useless to try anymore.

Eleven months of marriage, followed by a brief

eleven days of anger and recrimination and more tears than she thought one body could hold. And then nothing.

She had come back from her first day of class to find Stefan's family gathered in their little apartment, quiet for once, packing and bundling all Stefan's belongings into the rented truck. No word to her the entire time, not even a note from Stefan to explain or just say farewell. She had stood mute and accepting, knowing there was no way she could fight against so much shared hostility and anger.

Four months later Gina had been the one to call and tell her that Stefan was dead. Which was the only way that Angie would have ever known, as there had been no word from her absent husband or his family since he had abandoned her. Gina passed on the news, then cried with her over the phone and told her when the funeral would be held and cried with her some more. And ever since then, for these past six years, they had marked each anniversary by meeting together at Stefan's grave. It was the only contact Angie kept with all her early dreams.

Gradually, as though the volume knob on a radio was slowly being turned louder, Emma's voice invaded her reflections. "Her father comes into the store from time to time."

Angie did not know whether to be grateful for the interruption or not. "Who?"

Her friend glanced over. "You haven't heard a single word I've been saying, have you?" Before Angie could protest, Emma turned back to the road and went on, "I was telling you about Carson Nealey, Melissa's father. He'll be in and out in the blink of an eye, loading up things for his garden and plunking down his money and leaving. Doesn't say hardly a word to anybody. He'd be a right handsome fellow if he wasn't so grim."

"I wonder if maybe I ought to meet with him," Angie murmured, glad now that what lay ahead could be pushed to one side. For now.

"Somebody ought to. Never can tell what that child is enduring," Emma agreed eagerly. She was happy to talk about anything and anybody, so long as there was the hint of mystery or gossip, preferably both. "I'll drive you by and keep an eye out."

"You'll do no such thing."

"Fellow like that, surrounds himself in mystery and silence, you can't be too careful. All anybody knows about him is he's taken over running the big shoe factory on the other side of town."

Despite herself, Angie was impressed. The shoe factory was the town's one major industry. "You mean, he's the new president?"

"The very same," Emma confirmed. "Haven't seen hide nor hair of a wife, though."

"That is a little strange," Angie allowed. "Maybe she still works down in the city."

"Locked up somewheres, more like," Emma offered and was suddenly off and running. "I've seen his face, and you haven't. All pinched and squinty-eyed, like a mean old weasel. Wouldn't be surprised to hear he's got her tied in the cellar, feeds her through the keyhole."

"That is quite enough, Emma."

But when Emma had the bit between her teeth, she wasn't that easy to stop. "And that poor sweet little tadpole of a daughter, probably keeps her on a diet of rainwater and cold grits. That's why she's so little, don't you know. Half-starved little thing. They oughtta lock up that mean old possum of a daddy and throw away the key."

"Emma Drummond, I have never heard the like." Angie stared at her friend in astonishment. "I declare, you are worse than a roomful of ten-year-olds. Where on earth do you come up with these things?"

"Inspiration and detection," Emma replied loftily. "Luke says there's a good dash of aberration thrown in there as well."

"Your husband has uncommon perception," Angie said from the heart.

"Luke says I can keep him better occupied than a double feature at the drive-in," Emma declared proudly.

"I can—" Angie stopped. The classical radio station Emma had playing softly began a chorale. "Turn that off, if you please."

"Why?" But Emma had heard the reason before and reluctantly did as she was told. "I sure wish you'd start back with the choir again, honey."

"That's one road I do not intend to walk down with you today." All through her teen years, Angie had been soloist for the church choir. Since returning from the university and the city, however, she had refused to sing at all.

"A gift like that shouldn't go to waste," Emma complained, almost by rote now.

"It's not wasted. I talk all day long in my classes. Sundays are my only day to stay quiet."

"That's not the same and you know it."

The state road chose that moment to take a sudden sharp turn, and there in front of them stood the stone gates and the sign. Angie ended the argument by pointing and saying, "This is it, Emma. Pull in here."

Emma's broad features lost their brightness. She steered the heavy Plymouth over to the side of the road. "Sure you don't want me to come in with you?"

But Angie was already climbing from the automobile. Even she could hear the flat coldness that had crept into her voice. "How long will you take in the city?"

"There's nothing in the city that's important enough to keep me from being here when you need me."

Angie glanced at her wristwatch but could not manage to focus on the tiny hands. "Two hours," she said, gathering herself for the long walk ahead. "That will do."

"I'll be here." Emma leaned her heavy frame

across the seat to better see Angie's tight face. "Just know my prayers are right there with you, honey. Every step of the way."

Angie had always felt the place to be not so bad, as cemeteries went, though she hoped and prayed she would be laid to rest back on the hilltop that had served their village for a hundred and fifty years. Numerous valley families had kin who had moved down to the city, and this had brought her to the main cemetery several times. The hillfolks' custom was to be present for all births and marriages and deaths, no matter if the ties that bound had been stretched thin as ribbons. No matter that letters might come seldom as Christmas, or that arguments might have driven the kinfolk away in the first place. All such things were set aside at the passage of human seasons.

Angie trekked up the steep slope, staying to the small side paths that wound their way through carefully tended lawns. She reached the crest of the rise and stood in the gray overcast afternoon. She recalled how it had been, those six years earlier, when Stefan's funeral procession had come into view.

In the distance the black shapes had unfolded from their automobiles and gathered about the hearse, their cries rising in the still air. Angie had found herself unable to weep, as though the noise from below had robbed her of the ability to express anything of her own. The wails had risen to a crescendo when the coffin had been shouldered. Angie had avoided the church service, knowing she could not possibly have endured more accusations and anger. She had remained hidden upon the hill-side, listening to the cries of anguish as the coffin had been lowered into the earth. Angie had gripped the limb of a nearby pine until her knuckles were white and had forced herself to watch. The air had been so still, the incense waved about by the black-robed priest had wafted up to where she stood.

Then to her surprise, in the silent void of a quietly exhausted heart, she had heard the prayer arise. A prayer of forgiveness for the husband who had abandoned her, for the family who had shut her out, for herself. And in the prayer had arrived the fragile beginnings of peace.

As the group had begun to drift back toward the waiting automobiles, Gina had turned and searched the hillside. Then she had bent over and pulled out a single flower from those surrounding the grave, before walking steadily up the hill toward Angie. Others had stopped to watch and had discovered the reason behind Gina's direction. Angie had fought back the impulse to turn and run. Instead, she had taken a deep breath, straightened up as tall and erect as she could manage, and stepped from behind the tree.

A low murmur had run through the gathering. Angie had watched Gina mount the rise, until she came close enough to reach out her hand and say quietly, "For the honor you have done both Stefan and my family. For the wrong they have done you in return."

Angie had accepted the flower with a whispered thanks, then looked on as Gina retraced her steps. She had stood there beneath the pine, the white rose held with both her hands, and waited as the procession wound its way back down the long drive. Angie had then dropped her gaze to the flower and finally found the freedom to weep.

The western hills remained shrouded in shared sorrow, veils of gray mist hanging motionless about the verdant slopes. Angie sighed and felt as though she were trying to breathe around a chest full of broken dreams. This was always the hardest part of her annual visits. The memories seemed so recent, so immediate when she came here.

And yet even here, even now, there was a sense of the same peace she had known when she had prayed at her husband's funeral. As though the prayer had been a turning. And in the turning she had received a gift that was to remain with her forever. The same comforting presence that had been with her ever since those first days of returning to the university and to God. Knowing that both moves were right. Knowing that she would be healed and that she would somehow find her way through it all.

When she spotted Gina coming along the path, Angie picked her way down the rise to meet her. Gina had her brother's dark eyes and hair, as did all the family. But where they were loud and bitter and held grimly to anger, Gina was cheerful in a matter-of-fact way. Little seemed to faze her, and what did rarely was allowed to for long. But as she approached, Angie could see how time had laced more gray within the dark tresses and etched more lines out from her smiling eyes.

"So. You came." Gina settled her bouquet against the gravestone, then turned and gave Angie a fierce hug. "You of all the family."

"I really come to see you."

Gina gave her another hug and one of her quick flashing smiles. "How have you been?"

"Fine. And you?"

"Four children and a husband, and now they have me in charge of the kitchen; how do you expect me to be?" Shrewd dark eyes inspected her carefully. "You do not look fine. You look like you are still carrying the past with you."

"In this place, what else do you expect?"

"Exactly, in this place." Gina guided her over to the marble bench across the path from the family's plot. "Why, I ask myself, does this lovely young lady come back year after year to this place?"

Such directness was Gina's trademark, but still Angie was not expecting it from someone she saw only once a year. Especially here. "I just said—to see you."

Still Gina persisted, "Why, I ask, does she honor the anniversary of a man who abandoned her in her hour of most desperate need? One who then died without making amends?" Her challenge hung in the air between them like a shroud.

Angie stared at the dark granite tombstone. "He was still my husband," she said quietly.

Gina took hold of Angie's hand. "You are a fine person. I do no dishonor to the family in saying the truth. And the truth is, Stefan wronged you. He wronged us all. On behalf of all my family, I ask your forgiveness."

"You have it," Angie replied, her eyes still on the grave. "You always have."

Angie could feel the gaze searching her face but did not turn back. Finally Gina asked, "You have found a man who deserves you?"

"No man. Not anymore. I'm not really interested."

"Of course you're interested. A lovely young woman in the prime of life is not meant to be alone."

"A lot of things in life aren't what they're meant to be."

"No." A sigh, a moment's pause, then, "But you are young. You have faith. Why do you not let the good Lord heal your wounds?"

"I think He has," Angie replied slowly, wondering at how she could remain sitting here, feeling such comfort in the presence of questions she would never have asked herself.

"And *I* think you still hold to the past and have

done so for too long." Gina opened her voluminous purse and extracted a card. "Here."

"What is it?"

"Something I read the other morning in my daily devotionals book. It's from a poem by Byron. The instant I saw it, I knew it was meant for you."

Reluctantly Angie accepted the card. A tingle passed through her fingertips and up her arm, as though the gift held some special energy. Some intended challenge.

"I pray for you," Gina said simply. "I pray that whatever shadows remain from your loss and your hardship will vanish, that the Lord will heal you fully. That you will *let* Him finish what He has already begun."

"Thank you," Angie murmured. Her fingers still pulsed, a quickening surge that drew her gaze. She raised the card and read:

> *"My very chains and I grew friends,*
> *So much a long communion tends*
> *To make us what we are—even I*
> *Regained my freedom with a sigh."*

"Now turn it over," Gina instructed quietly.

Angie did as she was told and saw the back was inscribed with a verse from the hundred and twenty-sixth Psalm: "They that sow in tears shall reap in joy. He that goeth forth and weepeth, bearing precious seed, shall doubtless come again with rejoicing, bringing his sheaves with him."

"I want you to do something for me," Gina said, her straightforward tone softened with concern. "Don't come back."

Angie tore her gaze away from the card. "What?"

"We can find a happier place to meet from now on." She reached over and patted Angie's shoulder. "Go. Go and finish your restoration. Go and start a new life. Too soon we will join all these others. Our bodies will lie beneath earth and stone; our souls will stand before God. When He asks us, 'What did you do with your life?' What will you tell Him?"

"That I tried," Angie replied softly and still felt the current pass from the card through her body.

"Yes, of course, you tried and you held to faith, and this is good. But did you try your hardest? Did you accept a full healing when it was offered? Did you serve your Father when He called? Were you everything He asked you to be?"

Angie sat and stared at this dark-haired woman and found she had no reply.

"Go," Gina urged her. "And the next time we meet, come to tell me how you have opened yourself up once again and *lived*."

It took far longer than she expected to recover from her visit to the cemetery. A full month passed, in fact, before Angie lost the sense of floating through the days, with all she saw and felt filtered by an unseen glass.

The only time the partition seemed to dissolve was in church, when Angie bowed her head and found peace. But when she walked back to her little house and saw the card and its message sitting there on the mantel, the confusion and tumult returned. Even so, she could not bring herself to throw the card away.

In fact, it was while walking out from church that she finally decided it was time to speak with her oldest friend about it all. That Sunday, Angie passed through the church doors and walked down the little stone walkway, savoring the day's surprising warmth. The winter had not yet penetrated the valley, nor sent the trees to their slumber. The maples and poplars and cherry trees all remained dressed in autumn finery, their gold mantles flecked with orange and crimson. In the distance, the highlands were brown and bare, and Angie had a sense of being shielded and protected in her valley town.

"I do declare, this is just the strangest weather." Emma came bustling over, sliding her hands into gray leather Sunday gloves. "Whoever would have thought that a November day could be this warm?"

Angie slipped her arm through her friend's and said, "Take a turn with me."

Together they walked around back of the stone-and-brick church, through the little communal garden that connected the parsonage to the chapel. As the river's chuckling song became audible, Angie said, "I never thanked you for taking me into the city that day."

"I didn't give you anything but chatter."

"Which was exactly what I needed." She guided them over to the wooden bench set at the riverside. "I owe you an explanation."

"You don't owe me a thing," Emma replied but settled herself onto the bench expectantly.

"Eleven months after I married, the doctor told me I could never have a baby."

"Oh, dear sweet child." Emma reached over and grasped Angie's hand. "Why ever haven't you talked to me about it before now?"

"There was nothing to be gained by bringing it up." She was pleased with the matter-of-fact way she said that. "Stefan took it very badly. He blamed me somehow. His whole family did. A little more than a week after, he left me."

"Hmmm, mmmm, mmmm." Emma shook her head. "I never did like that man."

Despite herself, Angie had to smile. "You only

met him once. At the wedding."

"Once was enough. All that shouting and running around waving hankies in the air—that was no way for grown men to act."

"They were dancing."

"Not to mention how they kept picking up those perfectly good plates and tossing them every whichaway. Piles of broken crockery in every corner—is that how grown folks should behave?"

"They break plates for luck," Angie protested. "It's a Greek custom."

"And those songs." Emma gave as delicate a shudder as her heavy frame allowed. "I declare, I've heard dogs howl more in tune."

Angie stared at her friend. "You're doing this on purpose, aren't you?"

Emma made a surprised face. "What on earth are you going on about now?"

"I remember very well how you danced at my wedding until dawn."

"I never."

"Your feet got so sore you left your high heels by the wedding cake. And somebody spilled punch all over them. And you were feeling silly enough to put those horrid, sticky things back on your feet, then kick your heels up so everybody could see how they were splotched purple." Angie nodded. "You're just saying those things so I won't feel down."

Emma smoothed a crease from her Sunday dress. "Angie Picard, I have known you since you were the only child who could fingerpaint without getting a drop of color on her frock. And I'll tell you something I've wanted to say for a long time. Ever since you came back from the city, you've had a mighty slow smile. It's as though each time you have to relearn the task, and you're not quite sure you got it right. But when something finally gets you going, you can smile with more heart than anybody I've ever known. And I think you need to start smiling more, my girl. Whatever you're keeping inside that holds you back from smiling needs to be put aside, once and for all."

Angie felt herself shaken by how closely those words resembled the ones that had come from Gina. She tried to deflect the issue. "I tell you about my husband leaving me and not being able to have a baby, and you want to talk about smiling?"

"Child, I've known all about this baby business for years. And you told me yourself about that mistake of a man the week you returned to town." Emma flicked at a slow-flying honeybee. "Here it is the week before Thanksgiving and the bees are still out looking for flowers. The world's all messed up, if you ask me. Not even the seasons know what's what anymore."

"Tell me how you knew, Emma."

The big woman turned to her friend. "Your momma, bless her heart, wrote me before you came back home. She was afraid you wouldn't tell me yourself, and she thought somebody needed to know, and she was right on both counts."

Angie slumped back, defeated. "Well, that's that, then. If you know, so does the whole town."

"I've forgotten more secrets than you've ever heard," Emma replied calmly. "So you can stop with your nonsense."

"You're the one who's going on with the nonsense about bumblebees and men with hankies."

"All I'm trying to say is, you're past time for a mending, dear."

"You make it sound like I've wanted to hold on to this."

"Maybe you have, at least a little, anyway. Seems like you'd have been better off telling me long before this, for one thing. Never did feel like I could bring it up until you did. Even so, sorrow is always easier to bear if you've got a friend there to help you carry it."

Angie felt the pressure of someone seeing more of her than she felt comfortable with. "I think I hear Luke calling for you."

"I'm not letting you go," Emma replied, hugging her friend close. "Not until you promise if you find yourself facing a bout of the lonelies and 'if-onlys,' you'll call me. No matter what the time."

Angie smiled around the sudden lump, nodded jerkily, and said, "Promise."

Angie stepped onto the unfamiliar flagstone porch and stopped to check the hemline of her dress. As the school's family representative, she had every right to check on students and their families. She stilled her nervous hands at her sides and walked toward the front door.

Developers had partitioned several of the gentler slopes rising from the town and drawn curving lines of asphalt. The houses and their modern designs attracted city dwellers looking for weekend retreats and retirement homes. The town was glad to have them, for they spent money as only city folk knew how.

The Nealey residence was a low-slung house of stone and glass, with a broad patio lined by a wrought-iron railing. A grand place without being overlarge, it possessed a stunning view of the valley and surrounding hills. Angie paused and looked behind her; the town stretched out beneath the star-flecked sky like a golden necklace.

Angie turned again to the door and lifted her hand, wishing she could overcome her reluctance about this visit. Life was seldom picture perfect, nor were families. She walked a careful line when expressing concern over a child, and she seldom made these visits without some clear proof. Still, she remained troubled over the quiet young girl.

Melissa Nealey had not broken down in class again, nor had Angie's other music days seemed to disturb the child. But Melissa's calm remained too fixed, her face too sad. Something was wrong, Angie knew that for certain. It was her responsibility to make sure it was nothing serious.

Angie stiffened her resolve with her shoulders and knocked on the door.

There was a long wait, so long she was wondering if perhaps she should return another time. Then suddenly the door was flung open with such force that she took an involuntary step back. A stern voice said, "Yes?"

"Mr. Nealey?"

"Who wants to know?" The porch light remained off. The inner room's illumination cast the man's features into lines and angles and shadows.

"My name is Angie Picard. I am one of Melissa's teachers."

"Oh." The man seemed to fumble for a moment, as though he had forgotten all his manners. "Just a minute."

He leaned away for an instant, and suddenly light flooded the patio. When he came back into view, Angie found herself facing a man who looked so stern his intensity was almost palpable. His eyes had retreated into their sockets and peered at the world with bewildered hostility. Yet beneath the stern mantle was a subtle handsomeness. Refined, intelligent features bore marks of strength. And of suffering.

His voice sounded metallic as he demanded, "Is something the matter?"

"No. That is, well..." Angie hesitated, then pressed on. "May I come in?"

"What?" He appeared startled, then grudgingly gave way. "I suppose so."

"Thank you." She stepped into a family room of almost monastic austerity. Sofa and chair and low table were set precisely, as though the angles had been measured and the places marked. The carpet and wallpaper and drapes were all warm toned and new and expensive, as was the big television and phonograph cabinet in one corner. But there was no sign of who lived here, nothing on the walls, no pictures on the big mantel, no flowers. It held all the warmth of a hotel room.

Angie chose not to seat herself. "I... Melissa has been absent a great deal recently. Nine days in the past three weeks alone."

Carson Nealey's face pinched tighter, and deep-seated bitterness took hold. "I am well aware of my daughter's health."

"It is standard policy to check up in such situations," Angie persisted, keeping her tone even. "Our records show that you have been the one to call in, reporting her sick. Does she have a chronic condition that we should be aware of?"

"My daughter is perfectly fine," he snapped. "And so am I. So I'll thank you to mind your own business."

"She can't be fine, can she, now," Angie responded, not willing to back down an inch. Something was wrong here. She could sense it in the air. And when it came to the welfare of one of her children, nothing could force her away or scare her off. Nothing. "Not if she's been sick more than any other child in my care."

"Your care," he spat. "You're a teacher, nothing more, nothing at all. She's my child. Mine."

"It is important that I know what is going on with Melissa, Mr. Nealey."

"First that meddlesome doctor comes sniffing around, and now you."

"Doctor Thatcher has been here? My records show nothing—"

"That's because I didn't let him poke his nose where it's not wanted."

"It is part of small-town life to show concern for our own," Angie explained. She was back on familiar ground here, able to hold on to both her temper and her position until she garnered what information she needed. "Especially for our children."

"She's not your anything," he lashed out.

"The law says otherwise," Angie replied. It was one of her traits, this ability to respond to anger in others with calm. "Could I perhaps have a word with your wife?"

For some reason the request brought a flush of new rage to the man's face. He shot a finger toward the door and demanded with quiet fury, "Get out of here. Right now."

But she did not budge. "If I leave, Mr. Nealey, it will only be to return with the sheriff."

"Make sure your warrant's in order," he spat out. "Otherwise I'll bury you and all your busybody—"

He was cut off in mid-flow by a small voice. "Shame, Papa. Stop that this very instant."

The man's finger dropped to his side. "What are

you doing out of bed, honey?"

"That's no way to talk," Melissa Nealey chided. She stood at the door of the room, wearing a flannel nightgown, bedroom slippers, and a cotton robe. Her face was flushed. "What would Momma think?"

Carson Nealey's anger crumpled with his resolve. "I... she..."

"Miss Picard is just doing her job." A very different child turned to face Angie, one who was truly not a child at all, but a very calm and steady young lady within an undersized body. "Now apologize to the teacher, Papa."

His eyes on his daughter's head, the man mumbled, "I apologize."

"That's better." She stepped toward the door. "Could we talk out on the patio, Miss Picard?"

"I... that is, yes, of course." Meekly she followed Melissa from the room, suddenly unable to meet the man's eyes. It was as though she had witnessed something too revealing about him, too personal, watching how he had simply faded beneath his daughter's quiet voice.

Melissa shut the door firmly behind them, then bundled her robe up tight to her neck with one frail hand. She coughed once, a weak sound, then said, "Please excuse my father, Miss Picard."

"Of course," she said, unable to respond to this strange girl as she would to any other thirteen-year-old. "It's just that I have been concerned about you."

"My father went through a very bad time three years ago," she continued in a calm, matter-of-fact tone. "Papa has not been himself since."

"I'm so sorry," Angie murmured. "I did not mean to intrude."

"I have weak lungs," Melissa pressed on, taking refuge behind a protection of practiced politeness. "Every time I catch a cold, it settles there."

"You should let the doctor see you."

"I've seen a lot of doctors." The words came automatically, as though they had been repeated a hundred times and more. "I'm keeping up with my schoolwork, though."

"Yes, I know you are." And it was true. Melissa's test scores remained near the top of her class. Angie searched her scattered thoughts and came up with, "Perhaps your father should see someone."

"Papa has seen a lot of doctors too," Melissa replied calmly. "They didn't help."

"Well." Of all the things she had feared she might face this night, nothing had prepared her for such a discussion with a person who was both a child and a mature woman. Though the words sounded inadequate even before they were spoken, she said, "If there is anything I can do, you mustn't hesitate to speak with me."

"Of course. How kind of you to be concerned. But I assure you, I am fine."

Again there was the sense of hearing words spoken by rote. "I'll bid you good night, then. I hope you're feeling better soon."

"Good night, Miss Picard. Thank you for stopping by."

Angie stayed where she was and watched as Melissa turned and went back inside. Through the closed door, she heard the rise and fall of two voices, the small light chiding and the quiet rumbled replies. There was no anger now, no sense of need or danger. Only mystery.

For some folks, Christmas was a tough time. Not for Angie. For her, Thanksgiving was the hardest season to endure. It had been right around Thanksgiving, those six years earlier, when her numbness had eased and the sorrow had struck. All the world had joined hands and given thanks, or so it had seemed, with the message blaring from radio and television and pulpit. The irony had been a bitter joke in a time when almost nothing had made her smile.

But it was not Angie Picard's way to mope. Instead, that Saturday she rose with the dawn and was ready to go long before her town awoke from its lengthy holiday slumber. She wore a simple brown dress, one that would have been considered tatty and old-fashioned by most of the people she knew. But for the day ahead, her clothes were perfect. Angie settled a little brown hat into place, picked up her hamper and thermos, and stopped in the front hall to place her inside thoughts into the crystal jar. Then she headed for the garage.

Starting her car was always a puzzlement, she used it so seldom. She preferred to walk herself everywhere in town and normally favored the con pany of someone else driving when she left her valley's shelter. But not today.

As she slid behind the wheel, Angie had to stop and think to even remember the last time she had filled up the tank. But the old Chrysler Windsor was as reliable as it was huge, and the motor started on the first try. It shook off the weeks of disuse with a series of complaining coughs, then purred contentedly, ready for the day ahead.

Her way took her straight through the quiet town. Most everyone was using the Saturday holiday as an excuse to stay in bed an extra hour or so. The late November day was fresh and clear, the sky a wash of palest blue. Heralds of the coming sun streamed overhead, golden beams cresting the ridgeline to spread like awakening fingers across the heavens.

Not far beyond the town's borders, Angie turned off the state highway and onto a county lane. The road was not the broad rushing torrent of the lowlands. It resembled a meandering mountain stream, full of unexpected turnings and surprises and delights. Angie pressed down the accelerator to crest the first steep rise and listened as the big motor rumbled at the challenge.

The map was open on the seat beside her, but she had carefully traced her way the night before and did not need to check it often. Besides, this was still fairly well-known territory. She liked using holidays for such journeys, as logging and mining traffic would be at a minimum. Her way took her through an old-growth forest, the mountain maples so vast they formed a tunnel through which she traveled. She came over the ridge, but the trees hemmed her in on all sides and kept her from seeing more than the road sloping down before her.

Angie drove for an hour or more, in no hurry, stopping occasionally for a short stroll into the woods or simply to admire the view when a break came in the forest. The day's purpose was as much an excuse for a journey as it was a quest. She passed through one highland valley after another, leaving the bustle and the crowds and the town's civilized ways farther and farther behind.

Her first stop was a farmhouse she had come to know well. It was very important, building a bridge into these close-knit mountain clans. Doors were seldom open to strangers, but almost never closed to friends. The family who lived here had a son who had left to study at the biggest seminary in the state and now pastored Angie's church. Angie had taught two of his own children, and through this connection had been invited into the homestead and the clan.

Mother Cannon was out on the porch and wiping her hands on her apron before Angie emerged from the car. "A good day to you, Miss Angie. Been wondering when we'd see you again."

"Hello, Mother." She started across the swept yard. The call of pigs and chickens resounded from out back. The house was redolent with the smell of baking. "Did I catch you at a bad time? I can come

back. I don't want to be in the way."

"Get yourself on in here." Her offer to depart was ignored, as she knew it would be. Mother Cannon held the screen door open for her. "You can keep me company and sample my season's tea."

Angie followed the old woman down the hallway to the big kitchen at the back of the house. "Is that blackberry I smell? And apple?" And cinnamon and brown sugar and clove. Mother Cannon's pies were known three valleys away.

"The grandchildrens have been out, having themselves a time, gathering the wild berries. Little Tommy ate so much, his mother had to dose him with castor oil and put him to bed." She stumped over to the galvanized wood-burning stove, a prize that would have fetched quite a sum from one of the antique hunters who scoured the hills. But Mother Cannon had cooked with wood and charcoal all her life and was in no mood to change. "Been a right good season for late fruit. Got a cellar full of jams and preserves. You'll have to take a couple of jars with you."

"Thank you kindly." Angie watched as Mother Cannon filled the kettle at the hand-operated pump by the deep sink, the one carved from a block of heartstone granite. Five generations had been born and raised beneath the old slate roof, each content to live with ways lost and forgotten by the fast moving world. "What are we having today?"

"Bramble tea, mostly. A bit of this and that added for texture." The old lady took down a trio of

Mason jars. She measured a pinch of dried leaves from each into a strip of cheesecloth. "Found me some peppermint growing wild just beyond the vegetable patch. Don't often see it this far up." She formed a pouch with the cheesecloth and tied the end with a long stretch of twine, then settled the pouch into a teapot. "Always did prefer making my own teas."

The kettle began to sing. The old woman used a towel, singed black, to grasp the handle and fill the pot. The room was instantly filled with the scent of wild flowers and outdoors. "Got all the kin 'cept Robbie coming in tomorrow." Robbie was the pastor.

"That reminds me." Angie pulled a manila packet from her purse and withdrew several drawings. "When I told Pastor Rob I was coming to see you, he said you'd like to see what your granddaughter's been up to."

"Well now, I am obliged to you." She poured out two steaming mugs, placed one in front of Angie, and settled herself into a chair. Eyes turned milky blue with age examined one picture after another. She looked at them in silence, taking her time, savoring each in turn. Angie sat and sipped her tea and watched. Mother Cannon had a country woman's way of setting time aside, stilling herself, taking things in deep. Only after each drawing had been examined twice did she nod and say, "That girl is blessed with a passel of talent."

"Her daddy says she's been accepted to art school next year."

"Don't think much of a girl that age going off on her lonesome," Mother Cannon sniffed, fingers tracing their way across one picture. "But you can't keep a child to nest longer than the Lord allows. She's been proper raised, so God willing she'll remember what matters when the city beckons."

Mother Cannon settled age-spotted hands one upon the other and looked at her guest. "When are you expecting to settle down and have a family of your own?"

There was something in the calm tone that granted Angie the power to talk without shame or regret. "I can't have children, Mother."

There was no pretended shock or pity in her reaction. Instead, the old woman simply raised her head to peer at Angie through the bottom half of her bifocals. "You talked to the doctors?"

"Three different ones. They all said the same thing." Angie sipped her tea, wondered at how a mug could hold both nature and solace. "I've just had to learn to live with it."

Mother Cannon sipped from her own cup, a quiet taste. "You ever given thought to a healer?"

"I tried them too"—and again she could speak with openness and candor. "Before I found out and my husband left me, I was prayed over and had my head anointed and had more hands laid on me than I care to count or remember."

The gaze remained steady, the face calm. "You given up on God, honey?"

"No," Angie replied quietly. "He's been too

important to give up on. I couldn't have lasted through all this without Him."

She nodded once. "I don't hold with those who say a miracle's yours by right. Leastwise, the miracle we might like to see happen." She rose to her feet and lifted Angie with a motion of her hand. "Been through too much, seen too much sorrow to ever accept that as the Lord's truth."

She took hold of Angie's arm and guided her to the back door. Sunlight streamed through trees stripped of all but the last few remaining leaves. Beyond the split-rail fence bordering the pens and vegetable patch, a rough farrowed field rose at a gentle pace to meet the steeper slope beyond. Angie followed Mother Cannon's gaze as she looked farther, out to where a pair of elms sheltered the old family graveyard.

A rusting iron fence squared off a segment of carefully tended ground. The central markers were worn to blank slates by wind and rain and years. Those closer to the lower edge were bordered by flowers and markers of still-fresh memories.

"All I can say is, the Lord has been with me in my darkest hour and my time of deepest need. Got more questions than answers and lots of things I hope to goodness will come clear when I go Home." Mother Cannon turned and walked to the corner cupboard. "That's not much help to you, I imagine."

"Words from the heart are always a comfort," Angie replied softly, leaning against the doorjamb.

The old woman rummaged a moment and came

out with a bundle wrapped in newspaper. "My eldest came across this in her attic. Thought it might be of use to you."

Angie accepted the parcel and returned to the table. Carefully she unwrapped the newsprint, until she found herself examining a small chest of pressed glass. She lifted the palm-sized lid and instantly smelled the scent of ancient flowers. It had probably sat in a forgotten bedroom, filled from time to time with jasmine and spices found growing wild up on the hills. "It's beautiful, Mother."

"Goodness only knows how long it's been up there." Mother Cannon lifted her cup for another sip, then turned to the stove and opened the heavy door. "They bought the Cooper homestead back when the winter took the old folks, and none of the childrens wanted to leave their citified ways. Been after them for ages to clean out those upper rooms."

Pressed glass, also known as Depression crystal in these parts, had been a favorite of country families for three generations. It was cheaper than genuine crystal and heavy enough to survive the use of years. This one was decorated with carvings of hearts within hearts. "Anything else they happen upon that they don't want, please be sure and let me know," Angie requested.

"I'll do that," she said, reaching into the oven and setting one pie after another on the counter to cool.

While the old woman's back remained turned, Angie reached for her purse and slipped several bills under the sugar bowl. She had learned long ago never to talk money with hillfolk who chose to treat her as kin. She rose to her feet and wrapped the little chest back in the newspaper. "I'd best be off, then."

"Heard tell the Hawkinses over in Mill Valley might have a spinning wheel for you. Take the road over the rise east of here, ask anybody how to get there."

"I'll do that. Thank you."

Mother Cannon followed her down the hall and out onto the front porch. When Angie turned to thank her once more, the woman stopped the words with one upraised hand. Her gaze rested on Angie with the quietness of one who had endured the test of patience. "I'm going to speak to you as one of my own. There's unwanted trials that come to us all. It's important at such times to remember that when I suffer, the Lord suffers with me. He touches me at a level beyond words and offers me more tenderness than a mother does her child."

She cast a glance behind her, as though searching an unseen hillside. "Beyond that, all I can say at such times is, I try. I try to understand. I try to accept. I try to love both my neighbor and my Lord. I try to stay ready for when His call comes. I try to be worthy."

5

Thanksgiving Sunday greeted Angie with the tickle of sunlight. She had to shield her face and roll over before she could open her eyes, it was that bright. Rising from her bed, she saw how the sun positioned itself to come through the one crack in her shade and fall precisely where her face had been. She stood by her bed a long while, held, without understanding why, by the sight of that single ray of light falling soft and golden upon her pillow.

The gift of sunshine lifted her spirits as she prepared for church, which was a surprise, as Thanksgiving Sundays were normally a trial. It was hard to hold to her quiet resolve and keep the memories tightly encased in her crystal bowl, while all the world seemed caught up in a holiday that meant nothing to her anymore.

But today was different. Why, she was not sure. Yet different all the same, as though it was going to be a good day whether she liked it or not. She even found herself humming a favorite hymn as she slipped on her coat and gloves and let herself from the house.

Halfway down the walk, Angie stopped with a sudden realization. She had left the house without

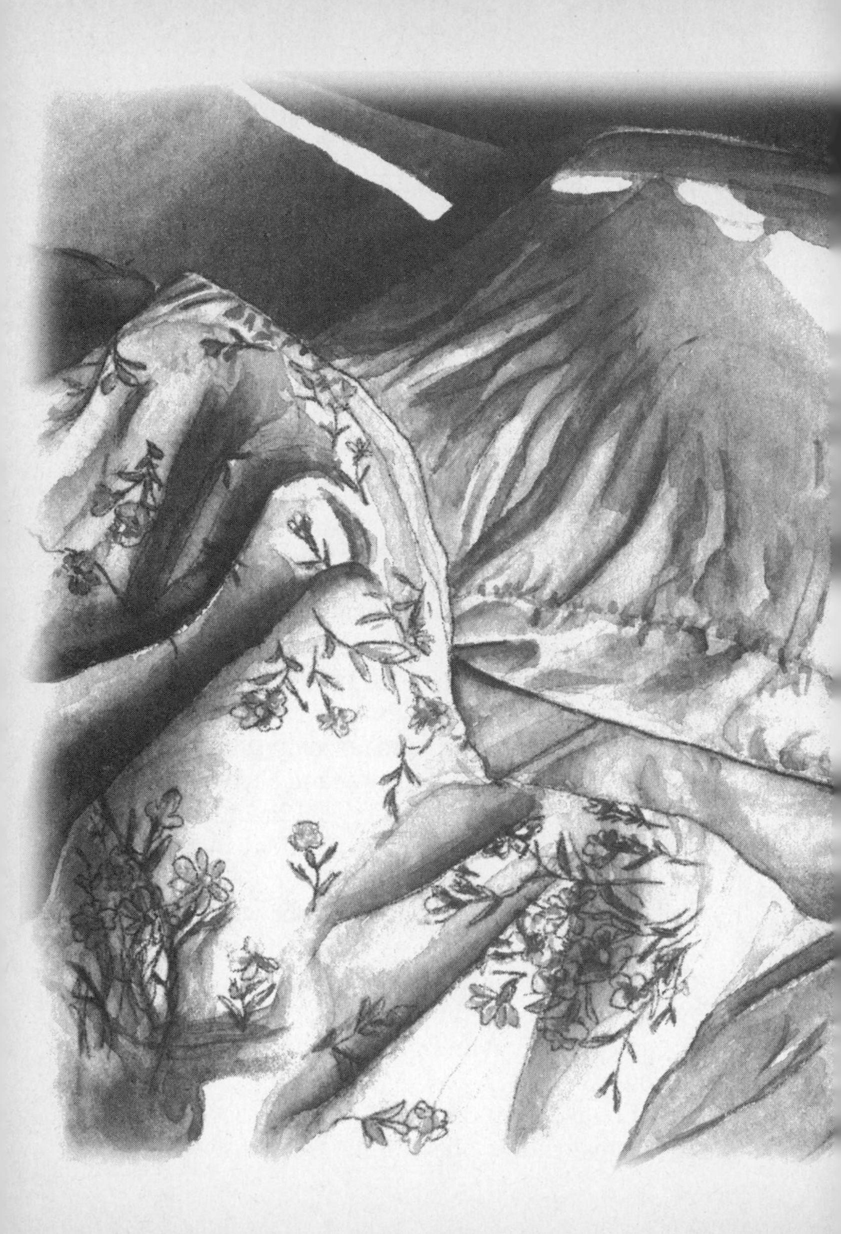

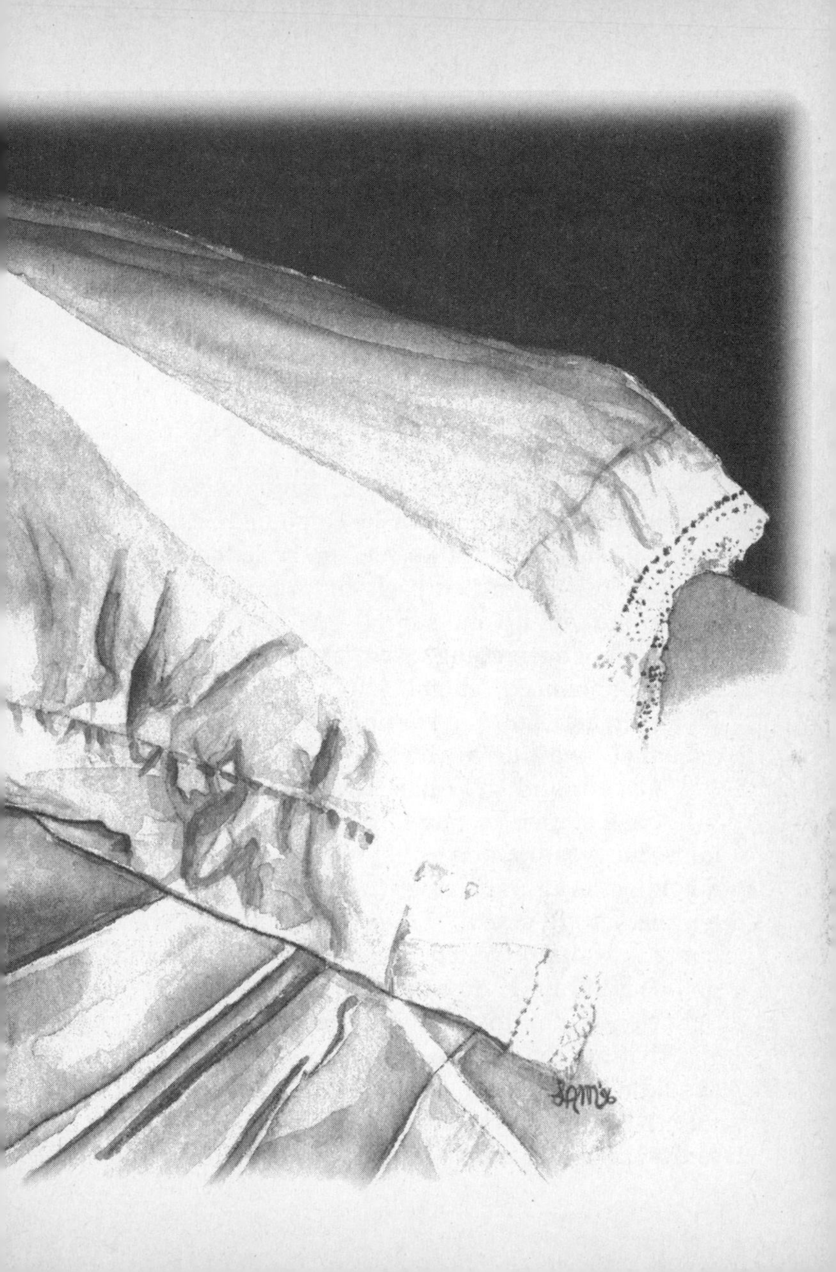

closing her inside thoughts into the crystal dish. The habit was so ingrained she could not imagine a morning without it. And yet she had done so.

Astounded, she whirled about, but as she did, the sun emerged from behind the sky's only cloud and struck her full in the face. Angie felt as if she had walked into a solid wall. The light both blinded and halted her. She turned her head and felt the sun's warm fingers keep her turning away from the house and moving toward the street.

Angie was baffled by this sensation which she seemingly could not resist. She continued on down the walk, but at the little gate she hesitated again. She would have turned back, but a car chose that moment to pull up and stop.

"I'm not even going to ask if you want to ride," Emma announced, climbing from her side of the Plymouth and shutting her door. "It's far too pretty a day to be wasting my breath."

"Good morning," Angie said weakly.

Angie started to raise a hand back toward the house but was stopped by her friend coming up and taking her arm and lacing it with her own. "Don't tell me, let me guess," Emma chirped. "You were going to walk to church and, along the way, see if you couldn't find some reason to drag a couple of dark clouds into this beautiful day."

That was enough to bring her back around. "I should never have trusted you with a single secret, Emma Drummond. Not a single solitary one," she said, slipping into their easy repartee.

"Then you'd have swollen up and popped open long ago. Because you keep more to yourself than anybody alive, and that's the truth." She pointed at the car. "Now go on and bid my husband a proper good morning so he can get himself on down the road. Deacons don't like being late on Sundays."

Angie nodded at Emma's husband. "Luke, if I have never said it before, I'll say it now. You are positively a saint to put up with this woman like you do."

The rawboned mountain man tipped his hat in reply. "You ladies have a nice walk, hear."

"Come on." Emma tugged on her arm as Luke drove away. "Don't want to be the last ones in on Thanksgiving Sunday."

"Why ever not?" But Angie allowed her friend to hurry her on down the road, though she did manage a single confused glance back at her sun-dappled house.

For some reason, the glance was enough for Emma to pick up the pace. "That reminds me. You know Louise Hollister. Her son Brant is in your class."

"Buddy," Angie corrected, having almost to skip to keep up with her friend. "Brant Hollister is a year younger."

"Whatever. She's a secretary over at the shoe company. You'd never believe what she told me."

"I know there's not a hope I'll be hearing it from you," Angie replied, lips pursed in mock rebuke. "You haven't been able to tell a proper story since kindergarten."

"You know that's not true."

"Emma Drummond, the day you lay out a story from beginning to end is the day I keel over dead."

"Now just hush up and listen. Last week Louise had cause to call long distance into the city to that big company, the one that owns the shoe factory. What's it called?"

"Allied Products."

"That's the one. Louise got to talking to somebody over there. And the woman, the one she was talking to on the phone, asked Louise how Carson Nealey was getting on."

"What?"

"There, see, I thought you'd like to hear. But oh no, Miss High and Mighty's got to go and bad-mouth her best friend, like she didn't enjoy a good gossip as much as the next person."

"You know good and well the only reason I'm listening to you is because I'm concerned about his daughter."

"Oh, and I suppose that means your earhole's any cleaner than mine."

"Emma Drummond, you are about to get a piece of my mind. Now tell me what the woman said."

"Well. It seems that Carson was one of their top executives. I mean, right up there. Then his wife passed on sudden like. One day she woke up with a headache, then just a few days later she was gone. Brain tumor. Nothing anybody could do about it."

"Oh," Angie said, the gasp pushed from her

chest, as though a giant's hand had suddenly reached out and squeezed the air from her. "That poor child."

"Poor is right. Seems both of them were just devastated. Carson fell to pieces. Didn't come in at all for a while, and then he never could work up a full head of steam again. Finally he asked to move someplace in the mountains, take over a small factory. And you know what, Allied never did plan on owning this shoe company at all. They got it when they bought a company somewhere else."

But Angie was not listening anymore. Instead, she was thinking about an undersized girl standing in the cold night, a mask of composure held tightly in place, doing her best to keep the family name intact. Playing at being an adult, while her broken heart sapped her of the strength to stay healthy. And for some reason, the memory caused Angie to think of herself and those lonely days of returning to the university after her husband had abandoned her, picking up the pieces of her life and her ambitions, taping them together behind a pale mask of her own.

Emma glanced her way, squinted at her face, and chose that moment to stumble. The heavy woman's weight was thrown rudely upon her, and it took all of Angie's strength and attention not to fall. "Are you all right?"

"I declare, this road's rough as a washboard." Emma stopped to check her heel, then tossed a shrewd glance at Angie. "You're worried about the child, aren't you?"

"I just said I was."

"And well you should be." Emma took hold of Angie's arm again and started off. "I imagine the whole story's just one big concoction. That fellow and his pinched weasel face, he's a wanted man, you mark my words. They probably shipped him off here just to keep him out of the law's clutches."

Angie had to gape at her friend. "I've asked you this before, but where on earth do you come up with these things?"

"Products of a fertile mind," Emma replied proudly.

Angie was no match for the woman's determined strength. "Will you ease up on my arm?"

"I told you already, we're going to be late for church." Emma did not slacken her grip until they rounded the corner and the church came into view. "I declare, you're worse than my youngest for finding reasons to darken a good day."

Sunday services were normally a time of respite. Angie was able to set aside almost everything for an hour or so and enter a quiet inner sanctuary that seemed hers and hers alone. Even in the worst of days, when the sorrow and turmoil had been such that she could not concentrate upon the songs or Bible readings, still she had felt this comforting hand of God. This to her had remained both a constant miracle, and a weekly assurance that in time the trial would ease.

Angie had never been given to outward expressions of faith. She had never felt an urge to dance her way down the aisle, or pray aloud for others, or lead a service. Yet in the depths of her sadness she had found an ability to connect with the Spirit, an experience so profound that she had resisted the temptation to turn away from God and give in to bitterness. Though her sorrow had remained hard to bear outside the shelter of shared worship, though the urge had often been great to give in to anger and hostility and enmity, she could never relinquish these moments of quiet reflection and inner calm.

But today was so different that she could scarcely concentrate on the hymn. Her attention remained drawn outward, as though the day was intent upon making her see the world beyond herself.

Pastor Rob gave the familiar call for a time of silent prayer. Angie again sought to turn inward, only to find that the pain was no longer there.

The realization startled her so much that she opened her eyes. The absence was frightening. She had lived with that gnawing ache for so long, now it felt as though something integral was missing.

Angie glanced around the quiet room, looking for something to anchor her thoughts and feelings. All she could focus upon was the brilliant sunlight streaming through the church windows. Great pillars of light, so strong they seemed solid bands of gold, fell upon the heads and shoulders of her friends and acquaintances. The illumination turned these ordinary people into beings of light and power. It transformed a simple country church into something holy, separate, divine. Here and now, this day, her sadness was not permitted. Her sorrow had no place.

She was so taken off balance by the day that Angie did not struggle when Emma invited her for a Thanksgiving Sunday dinner. Her ability to remain carefully aloof and isolated had been stripped away.

Angie allowed her friend to pull her toward where Luke and their two sons waited in the parking lot and again was struck by the power and warmth of the sun. She felt as though she had walked around for years with shades on, unable to grasp just how beautiful the world was.

As she stepped toward the car, Angie felt she was being given a message, one spoken to her heart, so forceful it could not be denied merely because the words were silent.

The message was four simple, powerful words:

Share Yourself. Share Me.

Restlessness came easily to Carson Nealey these days. Especially when he felt trapped in a situation going nowhere fast. Carson tried not to fidget, but this head office executive was dragging things out to an impossible degree.

"Got everything you need?" Carson worked at keeping any impatience from his voice.

"I can't figure this out, Carson." The man was a friend, or had been, back before his wife's illness. One of those who had urged Carson to stay in the city, work through his difficulties, and not lose his position on the corporate ladder. "You've increased production by twenty percent in four months! What did you do, stick a gun to their heads?"

"Nothing but a little applied psychology," Carson replied, wishing he could just get up and walk out.

"That won't wash." The executive flipped the file closed and put his reading glasses down on the pile of papers. "I want something solid I can take back to the board. They're going to demand specifics. You've already bought one new machine—why should they authorize any more?"

Carson sighed and settled back. He was the one

doing the asking, and this man had to sign off on his capital requests. "This used to be a good company with good employees," he began. "Loyal people. Some of them are third-generation employees. When the original owner died, that New York outfit bought this factory cheap and proceeded to milk it, pure and simple. Machinery was used until it fell apart. You've seen the production line."

"Like something from the stone age," the executive agreed.

"Then the war ended and demand for their cheap boots disappeared," Carson went on. "So the New York group got rid of it quick. They tied the sale to another company we wanted, forcing us to pay more than it's worth."

"I understand headquarters wants to go ahead and close it down."

"That would be a mistake, and the figures prove I'm right. Even with the dilapidated machinery, and despite the fact that their product line is fifteen years out of date, we're already managing to turn a profit. Now I want enough assets to build a new, high-quality line. Our costs are low enough to compete with these new imports, and our standards are higher."

"Listen to you," the executive marveled. "You're acting like this backwater outfit really matters."

"It does to them," Carson shot back. "And maybe it does to me. This is the town's only manufacturer. Let things go on like they are, the firm will go bust, and unemployment around here will triple."

"No, I mean, here you are, worried over three hundred jobs, when before you used to manage something like ten times that."

The personal observation brought Carson out of his seat. "I've got to get downstairs. We're expecting delivery of the new stamper this morning. Tell me you're going to sign off on the capital injection."

"Sure, sure." The executive picked up his glasses, flipped them back and forth. "No problem. But I've got to tell you, Carson, this has got people talking."

"Let them."

"Things like, Nealey's lost himself out in the back of beyond," the executive warned. "You stay here much longer and you'll have a tough time finding a place back at head office."

Carson grabbed his coat off the chairback and headed for the door. "See you in a couple of hours."

"Yeah, I got enough to keep me busy that long. Say . . ."

But Carson was already past his secretary and heading down the hall. He pushed through the reinforced door and stepped onto the catwalk. To his right was the glassed-in office of the production supervisor. Carson returned his wave and started down the metal stairs.

He had come to love the wide-open production hall, with its clanging noises and pungent smells of oil and hot steel and leather. The people greeted him calmly now, with the hillfolk's quiet acceptance. They were accustomed to him being around—not to inspect but rather simply to be a part of their work. In truth, it was what they had always been used to, up until the company had been purchased by the New York conglomerate. Before, managers were expected to spend as much time on the line as they did in their offices. Then the old owner had died, and the city executives had moved in, and the door at the top of the catwalk had only opened to deliver bad news.

But Carson Nealey had known none of this when he had arrived. He had come down to the floor simply because it was a way of keeping busy. Working with his hands, learning the business from the ground up, filling his mind with the twanging voices of the hillspeople and the banging, rattling sound of the machines—it had kept his mind too full to think.

Nowadays, there were few of the bad days, but his original habits stayed with him. He found that he liked the work, liked the satisfaction of a well-made pair of shoes coming off the line, liked the simple strength of the people employed here.

Carson joined the small gathering around the loading platform and ignored the slightly guilty glances tossed his way. There was no need to say anything. They would not stay away from their work for long. In fact, it was important they come and see for themselves as the tall crate was being dismantled and the packing stripped away, to reveal the gleaming new stamping machine. The first new machine to arrive here in nine years. Carson heard voices murmur over the cost—ninety thousand dollars—and wanted to tell them about what he was arranging—a credit line for an entire new production line. Almost half a million dollars to be spent over the next eighteen months. But now was not the time. For the moment, it was enough to see the reassurance and the pride they were feeling, that this new boss believed in them and their work and was investing in their future. A future he shared. Because as far as Carson was concerned, he was never going back to the city again. Not ever.

It struck him then, as it had many times over the past week. He found himself flung back to the night Melissa's teacher had come by. And once more he felt the flush of shame over how he had acted. But of all the nights for her to arrive, of all the nights to confront him with anything.

Carson tried to force away the memory by grabbing a crowbar and attacking the crate. Chuckles rose from the gathering at their boss working like a stevedore unable to contain his impatience. But Carson scarcely heard them. For despite his efforts, this time the thoughts would not be banished.

He did not have many bad nights anymore. Most of the time, he simply lived with a void. His heart usually felt as if it were filled with cold ashes from a fire long gone out. But the night the woman had come by, that was different. It was three years to the day since he had heard that his wife was dying.

The news had been so stunning, he had little memory of actually hearing the doctor's voice. For the life of him, he could remember almost nothing about the hospital at all. Only a few words had pierced his numbness, quiet words that had struck at him like hammer blows—tumor, inoperable, hopeless, not long. Four days later, she was gone.

The night Melissa's teacher had stopped by, he had been caught up in the feelings from before, all the rage and pain and helpless frustration. He had struck out at her for no other reason than because she was there.

But now, the shame would not let him be. That plus the memory of how she had stood there before him, the small mountain lady with the pale eyes, appearing so fragile as to bend in the slightest breeze. And yet she had stood up to his wrath, refusing to budge, defiant in her quiet country way. And all because she cared for his daughter—the one person who gave him a reason to not allow his life to fully unravel.

Carson Nealey stepped back from the crate, his chest heaving. He wiped at the sweat on his brow, wishing there was something he could say, some way to apologize and explain. But he never had been any good with words. He joined the group in exclamations over the efficient new machine.

Angie sat at her desk, the sheet of paper held in both hands. The empty room seemed to echo with the recently departed students. She sighed her way around to the window, sat staring at nothing for a time, and then looked back at the paper again.

It had long been her habit to follow a test with some exercise that would lighten the mood. All people needed restoring after a tough time. The issue was how to help the children accept the discipline of learning, while also pushing them to stretch their wings and learn to fly. Angie had neither the presence nor the confident strength of many of the other teachers. Yet the students took to her. Even the wildest children calmed down and did their best to listen. And she, in return, bestowed on them the love and the enthusiasm for learning which she yearned to give.

Angie glanced at the paper in her hand. Her heart felt squeezed by the words. The class had been instructed to think over all the cultures and places they had studied so far that year and then select a profession and a place and a time to practice it. Anything at all, anywhere in the world. If they wanted to stay here, she had informed them, that was fine, so long as they could explain what it was that held them. There was no right answer, she had said over and over. What was important was that they use this time to explore their minds and hearts.

Once more she looked over the page. Melissa Nealey's name was neatly printed in the top right corner. The writing was precise, the loops big and distinct, the *i*'s dotted with little round circles. All the signs of careful thought, a quiet little girl who had done exactly as the teacher had instructed, and who had plumbed the depths of her soul. But her answer. Angie heaved a deep sigh. Oh, her answer.

> *My favorite job in the whole wide world is not in the world at all. I would like to go to heaven and be the person who collects all the balloons that have floated out of children's hands and disappeared. When I was little I lost a balloon at the county fair. It was the last summer my momma was well. When I started to cry, my daddy told me all the balloons wanted to be close to God, and when we let them go, they went up and made God happy. So he explained that I shouldn't cry.*
>
> *I would collect them and give them out to all the children who have been called home early. And I would live with my momma, who left me and Daddy three years ago when God called her home.*

There was a quiet knock at the door, then it pushed open with a creak. "Miss Picard?"

"Melissa." Swiftly Angie set down the paper, as though caught doing something wrong. "What are you doing still at school?"

Timidly the girl entered the room, walked over and stood near the desk, fidgeting with her bookstrap. "I was wondering if I could have my assignment back."

Angie studied the slight figure and asked, "May I ask why?"

A moment's hesitation, then, "I've changed my mind. I'll do another one tonight and turn it in tomorrow."

Angie gave a slow nod and handed the paper over. "I have to tell you, Melissa, I've already read it."

The little shoulders slumped. "Daddy says we need to stop thinking about it."

"What, about your mother's death?" Angie leaned over and slid a chair closer to her desk. "Sit down here, Melissa. Why did he say that?"

"He says we've grieved enough. I think he's right, too."

Angie searched carefully for the proper words. "Have you really had a time to be sad?"

There was no hesitation to her response. "I feel like I've cried all the tears the world can hold."

The words seared like a red-hot knife. Angie tried to keep her face calm and asked, "You still miss her, don't you?"

A single nod, the words almost a whisper. "So much."

It struck her then, a knell that echoed through her with a force so powerful it did not need to be heard. The message came to her again. *Share Yourself. Share Me.*

It would have been easy to drape the message in all her past hurts and push it aside. So very easy. Yet there was something that held her, some sense of being drawn into an act and a moment that held far more importance than she could fathom.

The moment stretched on. Angie remained caught not by indecision but rather by the sense of being called to service. Melissa sat and kicked her legs in forlorn jerks, her face downcast.

Then another thought struck Angie. She pulled open her bottom drawer and brought out a bundle wrapped in old newspaper. She had taken the glass chest home but could not seem to find the proper place for it. So she had brought it to school, thinking it could hold her paper clips and rubber bands. But then it seemed too nice for such a commonplace use. Now that she looked at it again, she had the feeling that it had held another purpose all along.

"I want you to have this," Angie said quietly.

The girl's eyes grew wide. "For me?"

"Be careful," Angie replied. "It's very old."

Cautiously Melissa unwrapped the newspaper. When the heavy lead glass came into view, her smile transformed her face. Melissa fit the lid onto the base, held it up, and watched as the sunlight turned the pressed glass into a glittering box of prisms.

"Look, it's catching rainbows!" Suddenly the serious girl was a child again, so excited she could no longer sit still. She bounded up and danced over to the window to hold the box up so that the light fell strong upon it. "Look, Miss Picard! It's a box for rainbows, and it's got hearts all over it!" She spun around. "Is this really for me?"

"If you like it," Angie said. "It's yours."

"It's so beautiful." She turned back to the window and lifted the box back up. "Momma used to love boxes too."

For some reason the matter-of-fact tone brought a burning to Angie's eyes. She swallowed, then said, "Did she now."

"Yes, ma'am. Boxes and music. I remember how she used to say that everybody needed to collect some favorite thing, and she was extra lucky because she had four favorites, two things to collect and two people to keep." Slowly the box was lowered. "I get scared sometimes that I'm going to forget things like that."

"I am absolutely positive," Angie replied slowly, "that you are going to remember all the good things, all your life long."

Melissa looked back at her then, her expression now desperate. "Really?"

"Really." Again the silent chiming message resounded through her. Angie responded by asking, "What do you do with your Saturdays?"

"Nothing much." The girl's attention returned to her little glass box. "Daddy works, so I do my homework and read and maybe go for a walk or something."

"Don't you have any friends?" When Melissa responded with a little shiver of a head shake, Angie asked her, "Would you like to go for a drive?"

Again there was the round-eyed astonishment. "With you?"

On Saturday, the weather was with them. The autumn's first hard frost gave way to a pristine morning of brilliant blue. Angie had risen long before dawn and was ready for departure two hours earlier than scheduled. When she had wiped a spotless kitchen cabinet for the second time and polished the living room furniture, she forced herself to sit down at the kitchen table. She fiddled with her gloves and watched the clock's hand crawl around, rising twice to check if it had stopped.

Before she pulled her big Chrysler into the Nealey drive, Angie hesitated by the entrance to ensure that Carson had already left for work. When she saw that the way was empty, she started in, only to halt a second time. The sparrow of a girl hurried out to meet her, dressed in dark blue with a matching small-brimmed hat.

Her auburn locks were brushed until they shone, bouncing and flying out behind her with each excited step. "I locked the door top and bottom. And Daddy gave me money for lunch. And he says thank you. And you must come over some time so he can meet you proper." Melissa halted by the car window, breathless with excitement. "I think

I've remembered everything."

"You look perfect," Angie said quietly. "Come around and get in."

She did as she was told. Once Melissa was settled, Angie asked, "Can you read a map?"

"A little. Not very well."

Angie spread out the road map and traced a slender blue line. "We're going up into the foothills. I am beginning to make friends up there."

"We're going to visit friends?"

"In a way. I collect antiques. It's my hobby. These mountain people are very closed to outsiders. But they talk with me. Some of them, anyway. And if they have something they don't want anymore, sometimes they let me buy it." Melissa was watching her with bright-eyed enthusiasm. "Do you know what an antique is?"

"Something old. Like the box you gave me. Papa didn't want to let me keep it at first. And he said I couldn't go for a drive with you. He said it wasn't proper. Then I told him what you said about being able to remember Momma, and he got all quiet for a while. Then he said I could keep the box and come with you today." She turned her attention to the front window. "Daddy misses Momma a lot."

"I'm sure he does." Angie put the car into gear, and as she drove out of town, she wondered at what she could say to change the subject. But just as swiftly, there was an answering chime within her heart. *This was on the child's mind, something she could not speak of at home*. Perhaps she should follow the child's course.

As she turned off the main highway and onto a narrow county road, she asked, "Were the old folk songs your mother's favorites?"

"Momma had lots of favorites." Carefully Melissa lifted off her blue hat and set it on the seat between them. "She liked lots of old music, and she liked hymns, and she liked bluegrass music. She said bluegrass music was the best music ever made for tapping your foot. Momma said every time she heard bluegrass she wished she had a long skirt on so she could lift it up and whirl around the room."

Angie could only glance over once in a while, as the road twisted and turned and climbed at a steep pace. "Your mother liked hymn singing?"

"Yes." But something about the question left Melissa eager to talk about something else. "Momma said her old music was for quiet times, when she could sit still and take it in deep. I could always tell when Momma was in a quiet mood, 'cause I'd come home and she'd be playing old music with the big orchestras and lots of violins."

"That sort of music is called classical," Angie said. "Who were some of her favorite composers?"

"She had one she used to play a lot. But I never could say the name. I remember the story, though, the one the music was written about. Once upon a time there was a beautiful lady. She gets caught by a bad old king, who says he's going to kill her. But she keeps telling him these beautiful stories, and every night he lets her live another day so he can hear one more. Finally he falls in love with her, and

they get married and live happily ever after."

"Scheherazade," Angie replied. "It's a symphony by Rimsky-Korsakov."

"That's the one," Melissa said, nodding in her excitement. "Do you like it, too?"

"Very much. The music captures the feeling of struggling against terrible odds and overcoming them in the end."

"My momma struggled," Melissa said. "But she didn't win."

"You don't know that." Angie paused to choose her words with great care. "She didn't live, no, that much is true. But she left behind a legacy of love and a beautiful daughter. And from what you said, she met her Maker with great love and great faith."

When Melissa did not say anything, Angie asked, "Why did you and your father move here?"

"Papa said we were wasting our lives."

The words wrenched at her heart. Angie crested the rise, signaled, and pulled off the road. She focused her full attention on Melissa. "What did h mean, dear?"

"He said that a lot after the funeral." Melissa gaze remained directed out the front windshield. "B then he was talking about Momma. 'What a was he'd say, over and over and over. 'What a waste used to dream those words. Then for a while stopped saying them. And then last spring he sta saying it again, but he was talking about us now were wasting our lives. We needed to move or needed to go somewhere else and start over aga

"So you came here," Angie said, but inside she was remembering the night of the argument with the pinched-faced man. She had seen him as both angry and menacing. She had even feared for this little girl living with him. She had seen no seed of love in him, none at all. And now she felt mortally ashamed. "Your father is a very strong man. And wise."

"I think so too. Papa needed to come. I didn't want to, though. I was scared."

"What frightened you?"

"I was afraid that maybe if we moved I'd forget Momma." She turned imploring eyes toward Angie. "That's not wrong, is it?"

"I am sure your mother is very proud of you and of the love you hold for her memory," Angie replied. She watched Melissa settle back, as though the reassurance made everything all right. Once more Angie felt the gentle urgings of her heart. She marveled at this, for it had been so long since her heart had spoken at all. She led the talk back around by asking, "You say your mother loved hymns. Was she a Christian? Did she believe in God?"

Melissa responded by turning back to the windshield and giving a single nod.

Angie searched her heart for what needed to be said. "And you and your father, you moved away from God after she passed on?"

"Why not?" Melissa replied to the window. "God didn't do anything for us."

Angie sighed. And nodded. A very slow nod,

one of shared pain and understanding. She had been along this very same route. It would have been so easy to have abandoned faith, to have used her distress and her anger, yes, *anger at God* as a reason for turning away.

Slowly Melissa swung around, as though her gaze was drawn against her will. She watched Angie a moment, then asked, "Do you believe in God?"

"I do."

"But why?"

Angie could not help but feel the pain behind that question. And the yearning. Even so, all the words she had come to know from youth about salvation and repentance and commands, they did not seem to fit. So all she said was, "Because I could not go on without faith. I would have shriveled up and blown away a long time ago."

Melissa gazed at her with eyes that held both the openness of youth and the ancient wisdom of suffering. "Did somebody die?"

There was no place for anything less than the truth. "My husband. A little over six years ago."

Melissa stared out her window a long moment. "Then, you know," she said simply. "I prayed a lot when Momma got sick. I prayed all the time. And still God let her die. The preacher said she was in a better place. But why did God have to take her? Momma didn't want to go. She told me. She said if she was not already dying, the pain of not being able to watch me grow up would have killed her stone-dead." Melissa wiped an impatient hand across her cheeks, as though not wanting to take the time for tears. "Why did God make her go away?"

It came to her then—the Bible passage, and the need to talk it through. "I asked myself the same questions. I searched everywhere for answers. I asked everybody I could. And it seemed to me that the people who talked didn't know the first thing about suffering. And the people who knew, they didn't talk at all."

Angie turned in her seat so that she could face the young girl straight on. "So I started reading the Bible more than I ever had before, looking for my own answers. It was either that or close the Book and never open it again. And I came across the shortest verse in the Scriptures.

"A close friend of Jesus became ill, a man called Lazarus. By the time Jesus arrived, though, Lazarus had been dead for three days. All the family and friends were gathered about, crying and weeping and full of grief. And you know what Jesus did?"

"He healed His friend," Melissa said. "But He didn't heal my momma. Even after I asked Him. And Momma loved Jesus. I know that."

"I believe you," Angie replied solemnly. "But let's go back to the story for a moment. Before Jesus brought His friend back to life, He did something else, and this something is the shortest verse in the Bible, just two words. The Bible says, 'Jesus wept.' When I came to that passage in my searching, I stopped. I couldn't go any further. Why did

He weep? I wondered. The Bible doesn't say. Jesus didn't tell us why He cried. I thought and thought about that. And I decided that Jesus didn't say anything because He was a fellow sufferer. He knew He was going to die on the Cross. He carried this knowledge with Him all His life. He was born to suffer and die for us."

"So He was silent," Melissa said softly. "He knew suffering, so He didn't talk about it."

"That's what I decided," Angie agreed. "I don't know if I'm right, because the Bible doesn't tell us. But that's what my heart said to me. Jesus wept. Not for His friend, because Lazarus was going to be healed and rise up and walk away. No. Jesus wept for *everyone*. Because *all* of us who are born to this earth will suffer. It is a part of the burden of sin, of the imperfection of life on earth. None of us will escape the weight of sorrow. And because our gracious Lord understood this and because He loved us so, He wept for us. He wept *with* us. All of us. Even me. Even you."

Melissa's small chin trembled, and one tear spilled over to tumble down her cheek. She whispered, "I miss my momma so."

"I know you do," Angie said, and it was the most natural thing in the whole world to reach across, to take the small frame into her arms, to hold her close, so tight that the hat that had been set between them was crushed in the embrace. Angie sat and held the girl and let her sob and stroked her hair and shed a few tears herself. And somehow, despite the pain in her own heart, she knew there was a healing at work. Not just in Melissa, but in herself as well. She knew this because for the first time in years, she was crying not for herself but for another. "I know you do."

When Angie returned from church the next day, she found a strange car parked out front of her house. Then the tall angular figure emerged, and she breathed a quiet, "Oh, my."

But there was no anger on Carson Nealey's features. Instead, he awkwardly approached her and said, "Mrs. Picard, I hope I'm not—"

"Miss," Angie corrected. "I took back my maiden name. Melissa may have told you about … Well, anyway, you can call me Angie. The whole world does."

"Thank you." His face was not pinched, as Emma had described it and she had first thought. He had the sharply carved definition of someone honed down to his very essence. "I apologize for stopping by unannounced, but I wanted to say this in person."

"Won't you come in?"

"No, thank you, I don't want to be a bother."

"It's no bother. And if we stand out here in the street, folks will think either we're arguing or you're a bill collector working on the Sabbath." To end further protests, Angie turned and started up the walk. As she did, she breathed a fervent little prayer. Then she said, "It certainly is warm for this time of year, don't you think?"

"I suppose so." Clearly the man walking behind her was not comfortable with small talk. "Seasons seem more sharply defined here in the hills."

"Yes, Melissa says you're just recently arrived." She fought back a moment's embarrassment as they approached the house. She was seeing it through another's eyes, observing the peeling paint, the trim that needed replacing, the signs of neglect and wear.

But Carson Nealey apparently took no note of anything but his intended mission. "It's actually your talk with Melissa that brought me by. You see—"

"Where would you be more comfortable, Mr. Nealey?" Angie interrupted, determined to hold to proper manners. "Out here on the porch or in my front parlor?"

"I don't really mind," Carson mumbled.

"Well, perhaps we'd be better off inside. Even in the sunshine the air still holds a cool edge. Besides, I'm afraid I haven't kept up the exterior as I should."

Strange that she would want this man to come inside. Stranger still that the sense of inner guidance she had felt yesterday had returned. Angie entered the hallway, paused to take off her hat and coat, then led him into the front parlor. "Sit wherever you wish, Mr. Nealey."

"Please call me Carson." He stood in the high-ceilinged room and did a slow circle. "This is very nice."

"Thank you." Angie gave him a careful glance, searching for the politeness that covered disapproval. But his reaction seemed genuine. Which was strange, given the almost-sterile furnishings in his own home. She probed, "Some folks would say it's crowded."

"It's a home," he replied. He examined the polished oak flooring with its covering of hooked rugs, then glanced up at the crown molding that encircled the ceiling. "How old is this place?"

"Gracious, it must be a hundred and fifty years if it's a day." If she had any need for assurance that more than her own mind and heart was at work, she need look no further than right here, having such a conversation with such a man in her own front parlor. "Would you like a lemonade?"

"If it's not any trouble." He examined a mahogany sideboard supporting her silver coffee service and collection of figurines, then peered at a cupboard decorated with carvings of farm scenes. "You have some beautiful things."

"Why, thank you," Angie said, observing him through the open kitchen door. "I suppose Melissa told you antiques are my hobby."

"In a way. She said you liked to drive around buying old stuff."

Angie smiled at that, then explained as she poured two glasses, "Many of these country families still have pieces made by the original settlers. Some, like that cupboard there, are of great artistry. But many of today's farmers are the same as people everywhere—they want whatever is newest and brightest." She walked back from the kitchen and handed him a glass, then motioned him toward the sofa by the big bay window. "They know me and trust me, or at least some of them do. If they want to sell something, I'll either help them find an honest buyer or buy it myself."

Angie settled herself across from him and went on, "My parents bought this house when they first arrived here. They were originally from down Louisiana way. My full name is Angelique Picard. They've retired down to the coast. My father's had a mild stroke and isn't up to traveling. My mother has her hands full these days, but she's happy. She always did miss the sea. They left me this house." Angie offered him a smile. "My father worked as foreman at the shoe factory."

"Is that a fact?" His interest heightened perceptibly. "I'm just getting to know my people. The ones from families who've been there for two or even three generations—they're the hardest to talk with. But gradually they're starting to open up. I'll have to ask them about a Mr. Picard."

My people. There was something about the natural way those words fit him that appealed to her. "His name was Jason. Jason Picard. I'm sure some will remember him."

"I'll check on that first thing Monday." He set his glass down, clasped his hands, unclasped them, his face settling back into habitual lines. "Miss Picard, I owe you an apology."

"Yes." Angie tasted her own glass. "Yes, you do."

"Melissa told me about your losing your husband. I'm very sorry. Really." He pushed out the words in a determined fashion, as though they had been carefully rehearsed. "Do you have a time that is worse than others? I mean, a particular day when the littlest thing can set you off?"

Such questions from a stranger. She began to retreat behind her traditional barrier of prim haughtiness, to hold him off before he probed further. But something stopped her. What, she did not know. But it was not the time for standoffishness. Of that she was certain. She made do with a slight nod.

"Tuesdays used to be hardest for me. It was a Tuesday that Nancy's headache got so bad we had to take her to the hospital. Nancy was my wife's name." His gaze took on a dark, haunted look. "And it was the day we laid her to rest."

Again she started to reply, but was halted by a sudden flush of realization. Once more there was a sense of her heart silently calling out the now-familiar message. Yet this time there was no surprise, no resounding force. Simply a need for her to continue the service she had started the day before.

"I don't know what it was that hit me so hard the night you came by," Carson Nealey was saying. His hands moved restlessly. He crossed and uncrossed his legs, as though whatever position he chose was uncomfortable before he settled. "It's been months since I felt that way, like the littlest thing could push me over the edge. I know it probably sounds awful, but I don't miss Nancy the way I used to. Before, I felt like my heart had been cauterized with a red-hot poker. Not anymore. Most days, I just feel empty."

For an instant Angie found herself listening to the man and to herself at the same time. Hearing her own heart's silent call, to learn the lesson of love the only way it could be taught, by giving to another. Wondering if perhaps the reason she had not heard the Lord's directive in the past was because she had not wanted to.

Carson glanced up, his eyes as nervous as his hands. "I'm not saying this well. But I just want you to know that I'm not the way I must have seemed to you that evening. Not anymore. And I'm truly grateful for the friendship you're showing Melissa. She's talking about you all the time. She doesn't have any friends here. It's been harder on her than I expected—this move. I can't remember the last time I saw her smile."

He stopped then, his shoulders slumping slightly, like a balloon of tension had been deflated in his chest and he no longer had enough inside to hold himself erect.

Angie hesitated, not because she did not know what to say, but rather because she *did*. There was no question in her mind, no room for doubt. Not because it had been given to her in some powerful lightning bolt of the Spirit. There was no need. The answer was there in the same quiet assurance with which she knew she needed to speak.

When she finally did respond, it was to simply say, "Springtime."

That brought his gaze back up. "I'm sorry, what—"

"I am going to answer you honest for honest." Angie set down her own glass, settled her hands into a determined little ball in her lap, straightened herself fully, and said, "My husband abandoned me four months before he died, Mr. Nealey. We had been married just under a year when it happened."

"Call me Carson," he said quietly, clearly uncertain how else to answer. "Why—"

"I was informed by the doctors that I could never have children," Angie pressed on, amazed at herself. She needed to continue without pause, afraid if she stopped she would be unable to continue. Knowing without understanding how or why that this was not just correct, it was *essential*. "My late husband was Greek. When he learned that he could not have children by me, he went ..."

Angie had to stop and ease the tension in her chest. "My husband went berserk. There is no other way to describe it. I was already wounded beyond pain by the fact that I could not have children. To have my own husband verbally attack me left me absolutely shattered. When he left two weeks later, and died four months after that, well, to be honest, I didn't have much feeling left by then."

She stopped a moment to gaze out the window, then added, "Later, when the feelings came—the pain and even guilt—I sometimes wondered if it was my fault that he died. You know, his deep distress at the medical diagnosis...." She turned to face him again.

Carson Nealey leaned back in his seat, examining her with a totally new expression. As though the words had enough force behind them to actually open him up, push him beyond the emotions of his own heart.

But Angie was not finished. More needed to be said. "Whether it is birds or hyacinths or butterflies, in springtime everything is preparing for the joy of nesting. Everything is urgently focused toward that most important thing—new life. All else is subordinated to the need to create and nurture their babies. To make the nest, have the eggs, protect and feed the young. Feed the *children*. The power of the creative instinct is *everywhere*. It is the most complex thing in life, but also the simplest, the most natural. And here I am. The most sophisticated living thing in God's creation, and I cannot perform this function. I cannot act on that instinct. And I do have the instinct, Mr. Nealey. It gnaws away at me inside."

There was no longer the power to deny what was welling up inside. The heat of her words burned their way up from her heart, through her throat, poured forth with the message. "I feel so jealous sometimes. I envy how the rest of creation, everyone but me, can have offspring. I ache with the desire to do what I cannot."

Her hands were both damp and cold, clenched so tightly they felt incapable of ever unfolding. And yet, and yet in the midst of the pain of speaking what had gone so long unsaid, there was a sense of *rightness*. A sense that all had a purpose, even this, even here. "You must be wondering why I am telling you this. Melissa told me that you had turned away from your faith after your wife died. I have shared my sorrow with you, Mr. Nealey, because I need to tell you how wrong you are to do so. Not to have acted so then, but rather to abandon your faith *now*. And the only way I have a right to speak to you, I feel, is by showing you that in my own way I understand. I truly understand the temptation you faced and the reasons you turned away. Because I have faced them as well."

The man seated before her looked as though he had turned to stone. His frenetic movements had stilled. His gaze was fastened upon her, the gray eyes deep and open, as though it were not his ears that were hearing her, but his heart.

"In the darkest of my hours, I felt the Bible was of little comfort," Angie continued. "That is a confession I have spoken to no one else, but you need to understand just how deeply I feel for what you have faced.

"All through the Scriptures there is the command to be fruitful and multiply. But I cannot do this. And the inability to do this cost me my marriage. I am a barren woman. In the Bible, Sarah, the barren believer, ends up becoming pregnant. This is the way God dealt with barrenness in those holy pages. It leaves me with a mixed feeling, hope on one side, and disappointment on the other. I still hope, Mr. Nealey, I still pray for a miracle, I will not deny this fact. But I also know the medical facts. I am barren like another person is crippled and bound to a wheelchair. Jesus made *some* cripples walk, but nowhere in the Gospels does it say that He healed *every* cripple. He raised Lazarus from the dead, but He did not end pain and suffering and death forever. Does it mean that every believer should be healed and protected from suffering? I cannot answer this, not now. Perhaps in time, but not now. All I can say is that I pray about this as well."

Carson Nealey opened his mouth, closed it, swallowed, then found the strength to say, "And still you kept your faith."

"There was one day, a Sunday just like this one," Angie remembered aloud. "It came several weeks after my husband's funeral. I was in church because it was Sunday. I was going through the motions of a life. Almost without thinking. You must know what that is like."

"All too well," he murmured.

"When it came time to bow my head in prayer, I felt like I was falling. I do not know how it was possible to sit there in the pew and yet know I was falling. But it was as real as this chair I am seated upon. And everywhere was darkness. I felt as though I had passed through this endless chasm and out beyond sorrow entirely."

He gave a single slow nod. "As though there was nothing left to feel. Nothing at all."

"And yet," Angie went on, "there in the depth of my utter despair, I found God waiting. Not with an answer. I did not need answers then. I needed comfort. And that is exactly what I received. I felt the Lord enter my life and felt Him be with me there. He shared with me my sorrow, just as He shared with me my sin upon the Cross. He was there, and He has stayed with me through my long return. He gave me the strength to return to school and finish my degree. He accompanied me back to this town I love so, and He gave me classrooms of bright and eager children I can love and teach and help to grow and learn. God has been with me every step of the way. And He is with me still."

Angie waited a moment, as though offering him a chance to turn away, to refuse to accept what he must have known was coming next. But Carson Nealey's gaze remained fastened upon her, open and yearning. So she said, "That is why I have shared all this with you. Because you need to turn to the Lord and let Him be with you in your sorrow. You need this, and your daughter does too. You need Him to guide your footsteps, as He has done mine. No matter that He does not offer you the answers you would like to have. No matter that you are still in sorrow, even despair. Trust Him.

That sounds so simple, but doing so will profoundly affect your life. He will give you peace."

In the weeks following, there was no response from Carson Nealey. Angie decided he either hadn't understood or could not accept the truth she had shared with him. But all of life seemed held by strange and unexpected currents that year. Even the seasons were out of kilter, coming more slowly than anyone could remember. The first snowfall did not arrive until two weeks after Christmas, a Christmas which Angie had spent at her parents' seaside cottage, and which had held more bustle and talk and even laughter than she had known in years and years.

There had been snow flurries during much of December, quick little storms that painted brushstrokes of white across the upper reaches but did not touch the valley. Christmas was white only for the uppermost hillfolk and for those who hiked their way up slopes, made steeper by their frosting, to cut special trees and carry them home. But the second week of January, the clouds gathered as they can only do in the higher reaches. They closed the sky tight with frowning gray beasts of burden, their loads so heavy they drooped down to rest upon the peaks. The air turned still and cold, and everyone knew that winter had finally arrived.

School was closed for three days, a long time for a valley town accustomed to winter storms. But the snow fell so heavily that poor visibility made it hard to walk, much less drive. It was not until Friday that the town managed to reclaim the streets. Which meant that on Friday the students were nearly impossible.

"Three days of a world turned into a giant playground, followed by one day of school, followed by a weekend." Emma huffed her disgust at such bureaucratic decisions. She followed Angie through a lunchroom just a half-breath away from utter bedlam. "Only somebody sitting in an office ten miles from the nearest classroom would ever think that made sense."

Angie walked determinedly to the window table where a dozen teachers pretended not to notice what was going on around them. She put down her tray just as someone said, "What I don't understand is how they can eat and make so much noise at the same time."

"They're not eating," Emma replied, taking the place next to Angie. "They're foraging. Jungle beasts circling the kill."

The principal rose wearily to his feet. "As head animal trainer, I suppose I better go make the rounds."

"Speaking of noise," Emma said to Angie. "I had a little surprise this morning."

"So did I," Angie replied. "One of my students

slipped a bullfrog into my top drawer."

"Don't tell me you let something like that get to you."

"Not until it jumped about thirty feet straight up and came down in my hair," Angie said grimly. "Then I proceeded to put on a little show I am positive will keep them talking for years to come."

Emma smiled with the rest of the table. Then she said in a voice that could only be heard by Angie, "You remember that little girl I couldn't get to sing?"

"Melissa? What about her?"

"Nothing really," Emma replied, her tone overly casual. "It's just that I finally got a peep out of her. Since she's the only one in the class who knows the difference between musical notes and hieroglyphics, she's been turning the pages for the pianist. Then all of a sudden this morning she started singing."

"After five months of no sound at all, and you call that nothing?"

"Look at Little Miss Eager here." Emma obviously was delighted at Angie's interest. She squinted in the direction of the window. "So. Think we'll get the second helping of snow this weekend?"

"Emma, I have been looking to throttle somebody ever since my shimmy with the frog this morning. Now, tell me what happened."

Emma's smile broke through. "It was something, honey. I wish you could have seen it. There we were, a roomful of children doing their best imitation of two dozen cats caught in a burlap sack. And I'm standing there on my little podium, waving up a good breeze with my baton and stomping my foot like a pile driver."

"What were you singing?"

"Oh, some hymn."

"Emma Drummond, you are choosing the wrong time to test my patience."

"Amazing Grace," Emma conceded. "I thought a few of the old-timey hymns might calm them down. All of a sudden, this new sound chimes in. It was a shock, pure and simple. For a minute, I thought an angel had gotten lost and slipped inside our class."

Angie pushed aside her tray and leaned closer. "She has a nice voice?"

"You'll have to hear it to believe it." Heavy shoulders bounced at the memory. "I kept waving my baton for a time, slower and slower, on account of the fact that one by one every voice in the room had gone quiet. Could have heard a pin drop."

"Is this the truth, Emma?"

"Absolutely. You know those little silver bells, the ones that sound so pure you'd think they were fashioned in heaven? That's how she sounded. This tiny body, her head cocked over to one side, eyes closed, standing there beside the pianist who's the only one with enough sense to keep going but missing some of the notes on account of her eyes are on Melissa and not the keys. And she just keeps on singing, flying off somewhere and carrying us all with her." Emma's smile had a wistful quality. "Yes, ma'am, I do so wish you had been there to see it happen."

Angie was not sure whether she should say anything when her last class came bounding in. The little form slipped through the door, keeping to one side so as not to be caught by the boisterous revelry. But instead of heading for her desk, Melissa gave Angie a smile and walked over. "Good afternoon, Miss Picard."

"Hello, Melissa." The girl's evident happiness spurred her to say, "I heard something interesting about your music class this morning."

"It's been a special day," Melissa replied, slipping an envelope from her notebook. "This is for you. It's from Daddy."

"Why, thank you." Angie held the envelope and watched Melissa move down the aisle to her desk at the room's far corner.

She should have called them to order. She should have started the class immediately. It was the only way to handle such a situation. But their mood was infectious, and her own curiosity overwhelming. Angie lowered the envelope below the level of the desk and tore it open. What she read made her read it a second time. She looked up only when the noise level threatened to shatter the windows. She spotted what looked to be a key perpetrator and raised her voice, saying, "Mark Whitley, stand up, if you please."

The oversized youngster did so, struggling to tuck his grin back out of sight. Angie stared at him for a moment, then said, "Define 'decorum' for me, please, sir."

" 'Decorum' means, ah, proper behavior, Miss Picard."

"And that is exactly what I expect from all of you," she said, trying for sternness. "Is that clear? Very well, you may sit down."

The young man made a chore of slipping back into his desk. While his head was bent over and his face out of sight, he gave a remarkably realistic imitation of a very large bullfrog.

Angie then made a fatal mistake. She laughed.

Two of Mark Whitley's best friends actually fell out of their desks, they were laughing so hard. Angie tried to call the class to order, but she couldn't stop chuckling long enough to do so. And every time a student looked her way and saw her grin, their mirth rose another notch. Fearing the principal would come in and complain, Angie rose to her feet, which brought the din down a fraction. She raised her hand and demanded in as severe a tone as she could manage, "Mark Whitley, was that bullfrog your idea?"

"No, ma'am," came the reply. "But I surely do wish I'd thought of it first!"

She let them have another moment, then said, "It sounds like you all have heard about this morning."

Perhaps this was what gave the sense of a special place with her students, she thought as she observed their glee. Having the ability to share with them such things as a smile. Was that special? She raised her hand once more and said, "I think the wisest thing to do would be to consider that we've accomplished all that we can today. I'm going to let you all go early. Have a nice weekend."

There was a chorus of gleeful shouts, and as the students piled out, she stopped the tall youngster to say, "That was a funny-once sort of prank, Mr. Whitley. Do you understand what I mean?"

"Yes, ma'am, I think so."

"I would be most grateful if you would speak to the perpetrators on my behalf," Angie went on, signaling for Melissa to remain where she was. "Please inform them that my poor heart would not stand the strain a second time."

When the boy had taken his leave, Angie walked back and eased herself into the desk next to Melissa. She listened to the excited commotion of youngsters reveling in thirty additional minutes of unexpected freedom, made sweeter by the fact that all their fellows remained imprisoned. Before she could speak, the door opened and the principal demanded, "What on earth was that all about?"

"I have admitted defeat," Angie replied. "I could not abide their presence one minute longer."

He started to protest, then nodded acceptance. "I suppose I'd better do it for the whole school or risk mutiny."

His progress down the hall was greeted with a rising crescendo of unbridled joy. Angie smiled and found her heart twist at the sight of the sweet face beside her, beaming in response. Melissa's shoulders hunched up, as though the pleasure of smiling was almost too much to bear. Angie asked, "Do you know what your father has written to me?"

"Daddy wants to go to church with you and then have you come over for Sunday lunch at our house," Melissa replied breathlessly. "Can you come?"

"I would be honored. Can you tell him that, or should I write him a note?"

"Let me tell him, please, please." Her face shone with pleasure. "There's something else, Miss Picard." She had to pause for another breath before announcing, "We've been praying together."

"You and your father?"

"Every night. And sometimes in the morning, we'll read the Bible, if he's not already busy thinking about the factory. Daddy says he needs to do it more, too."

Angie opened her mouth, closed it, and then tried a second time. "That's just wonderful."

"I think so too. This was Daddy's idea, having you come. He says it's time we found us a church home. He asked me what I thought about asking you to take us. Know what I said?"

Angie just shook her head.

"I said I thought it was the best thing I could think of." Melissa slipped from her seat. "Daddy is going to be real excited to know you can take us. I just know it."

Angie watched the girl move to the door, returned her wave, and only when she was alone in the room did she realize she had forgotten to ask anything more about Melissa's singing.

10

Not even hosting visitors was enough to stop Angie's treasured ritual of walking to church. Especially not on a day when all the world was held in the silent white of winter's grip. Clouds had gathered again overnight, sealing the valley from above, making the stillness even more complete. The winter morning was a million hues of gentle gray. The occasional passing car seemed an affront to the Sabbath's peace. Her steps scrunched softly, and her breathing seemed loud in her ears. Here and there, tiny snowbirds appeared, their cheeps like chimes in the crisp air.

As she rounded the final corner, Angie spotted Carson Nealey emerging from his car. She hurried over. Melissa saw her and waved with such enthusiasm that her petite form seemed ready to take flight. Angie smiled and wished them both good morning.

"I am most grateful for your letting us join you like this," Carson said in a rush, the words rehearsed. "I have learned at the factory how closed this community can be to outsiders, and I was concerned that we might face this here at church."

"If you did," Angie said, feeling an echo of his

nervousness within herself, "I would be mortified."

"It was for that reason I asked if we could join you today," Carson pressed on, fidgeting with his hat. "I hope we haven't put you out any."

"This is God's house, where all are welcome, or should be," Angie replied, the formal words warmed by her tone. Then she glanced at Melissa. She was watching Angie with another of those smiles, the kind that were too big to be held just by her face so that she scrunched up her shoulders with delight.

Angie looked from one face to the other, then said, "I am honored that you would join me. Shall we go inside?"

As they approached, Emma stepped from the front doors. In her flowing choir robes she looked vastly impressive. Grinning from ear to ear, she said, "Well, praise the Lord! And who do we have here?"

"Melissa, you of course already know the director of our church choir," Angie said, her tone as cool as the walk.

"Yes, ma'am. Hello, Mrs. Drummond."

"Welcome to our little country church, Melissa. I look forward to having you sing with us some day," Emma said, but for some reason it was Angie who received the wink.

Despite strong efforts at self control, Angie found herself blushing as she went on determinedly, "Mr. Nealey, Emma Drummond teaches your daughter's music class at school."

"Nice to meet you, Mrs. Drummond."

"You have a talented daughter, sir." Emma cast her friend another look full of meaning and continued, "It might interest you to know that Angie Picard here also has talent and was the choir soloist for a number of years—"

"Why don't we go in before they start without us," Angie urged. Father and daughter entered the vestibule, but Emma grabbed her arm as she tried to pass. Angie was growing increasingly irritated. "Don't you have choir duties to attend to?"

"They can survive without me for just a minute." Emma's grin widened. "Are you ever in for a surprise."

"What are you going on about now?"

"You remember that friend at the shoe company's headquarters? She heard something else the other day."

Angie refused to let herself ask the expected. "If you'll excuse me, I have guests waiting."

"Something very interesting," Emma added, flouncing about so that her robes billowed around her. "But you're in such a hurry, I guess you'll just have to find out for yourself."

As with the town as a whole, almost everyone in church had some relative who had worked at one point or another for the shoe company. So to have the president arrive for Sunday worship was a cause for quiet comment. Angie attempted to discreetly trail father and daughter down the central aisle and reflected on the wisdom of accepting the invitation. Two bright red spots on her cheeks signaled her inner turmoil. *But after all,* she told herself, *I'm only introducing a new family to the church.*

Ignoring the eyes that followed their progress, Angie joined Melissa and Carson in a pew close to the front.

Together they sat through the first prayer and then rose for the opening hymn. Angie could not help but feel a little thrill as Melissa opened her hymnal and found the place without difficulty. Despite her feeling that Emma had been overly enthusiastic about Melissa's talent, still she was excited to see the child show such familiarity and interest in the worship time.

When the first verse began and Melissa started singing, Angie was so astounded she lost her place in the hymnal.

There was none of the piping, breathy tones of a child's voice. The sound was fragile, yes, but so clear it appeared to lift free of the earth.

Angie fumbled and found the line and started to sing as she had sung for the past six years, holding back, restraining from giving in to the music. But it was hard. With her open vulnerability, the girl standing between her and Carson challenged her to lift her own voice up in praise.

Heads were turning, glancing down at the girl, then at Angie, back at the girl, then around.

Melissa took no notice. She kept her eyes focused on the hymnal in her hands.

Angie glanced at the father and saw upon his features a sadness that twisted her own heart. He did not sing. He stood and watched his daughter with a look of love and sorrow. He seemed blind to the attention directed their way.

At the end of the first verse, to Angie's utter surprise, Melissa raised her head. She ignored the strangers watching her, looked up at her father, and whispered urgently, "Sing, Papa!"

He started at the intensity behind those words. Angie saw it happen. He straightened with a jerk, as though waking from a sleep. He looked down at the hymnal, took a breath. And he sang.

There was no longer any attempt by those around them to disguise their interest and curiosity. Carson Nealey sang with the graceful clarity of a natural tenor. The notes blended perfectly with his daughter, forming a graceful ballet of sound. He sang in harmony one step below her, taking the more difficult middle range, and became the platform from which she soared.

Angie watched and listened, and it seemed as though the chamber's light became centered on them. Not upon the pair standing and singing beside her. Upon the three of them. And in that moment, the silent voice spoke to her again. There in the Sabbath worship, in the midst of people she had known all her life, in the simple stone-and-brick country church, she heard the unspoken words resound through her.

Share Yourself. Share Me.

She did not need to read the words of the hymn. She had been singing them since joining the choir as a teenager. Angie closed her eyes to ward out the world, and she sang.

Gradually the long-locked inner door opened, as though her voice needed a moment to truly accept that freedom had come again. She tested it, using the first few lines as a scale, gradually allowing her voice to rise in strength and clarity. Angie felt as much as heard Melissa's voice shift in direction as she lifted her face to look toward Angie. But Angie did not open her eyes. She dared not. She was afraid that if she did and saw others watching her she would not have the courage to continue.

And it felt so good to sing again. So *wonderful*. Her voice seemed to find wings and soar, taking the third verse in joyous acclaim. Angie heard Carson's singing rise in strength, matching now not just his daughter's but hers as well. Gracing them both with a stage upon which they might pirouette in praise of the Lord.

Afterward, the congregation took longer than usual to settle. Pastor Rob gave the traditional welcome to visitors, then smiled down at her as he said, "It certainly is nice to hear our congregation holding such rich talent—both the new and that already known to us."

"Amen!" Emma's voice rang out from her place with the choir.

Angie hid from inquiring eyes by studying the

church program. Her gaze wandered over the page, before fastening upon one particular line. The pastor's voice receded into the distance, along with awareness of her own previous discomfort, as the printed words sank in.

The title of the day's sermon was written in bold type, five words that rose up to speak directly to her heart. She felt more than saw Melissa glance her way, but she was unable to return the look. Not just then. For the moment, she could see no further than the message upon the page, one she knew for certain was meant for her.

The title read: *Sharing Is Compassion In Action*.

"After my wife died, I didn't really ever turn away from God. Not specifically. I was angry at the whole world. I never bothered to single God out for anything in particular. He just got mixed in with the rest."

Angie sat against the car door, not to keep herself far removed from Carson, but rather to see both father and daughter without shifting her glance. Melissa sat in the seat directly behind her father and took in her father's words with quiet acceptance. Her face held a fading sorrow, like shadows cast by a sun lost behind thick clouds.

"The anger died after a while; I think it had to. Otherwise it would have consumed me. But I had a daughter to raise, and that above everything else kept me going." Carson drove with steady intent along streets ringed by white snowbanks. His voice contained a sense of departure, as though he was discussing a life that had belonged to someone else. "After a while it seemed as though I just stopped caring about a lot of things very much. Everything except Melissa."

"Are you happy here?" Angie asked, more because she felt it was time to speak than because she needed to know. In truth, her mind remained caught up by the scene after church. As they had started back down the aisle, almost everyone they passed had offered Carson a solemn nod and handshake. Angie sensed that it was not just because of his position at the factory. He was gaining a reputation, this man, for reasons she did not fully understand. These hillfolk were slow to accept a newcomer, and yet there they stood, thanking him for joining them in a way that had left Angie certain that they genuinely meant the words.

"Happiness is such an alien word," Carson replied quietly. "But to be honest, I think I would have to say yes."

A little indrawn breath from the backseat was swiftly stifled. Angie watched as Melissa observed the back of her father's head with wide eyes.

"I'm coming to love this town," Carson went on, turning into their drive. "And the factory. You can't imagine how nice it is to work with my hands again, to deal with issues that relate to people I know. Problems aren't just numbers on a balance sheet here. They are people and their jobs and their lives."

Carson Nealey cut off the motor and said in the silence, "If I never go back to the city again, it will suit me just fine."

As Angie climbed from the car, Melissa came around and asked, "Would you like to see my room, Miss Picard?"

"I think perhaps I should help out with lunch."

"You are our guest," Carson said, returning to nervous formality now that they were home. "Go on ahead, I'm a fair cook. I'll call when things are ready."

"Well, if you're sure." Angie followed Melissa through the front parlor, a room as void of soft touches as it had been the last time she had seen it. They moved through the kitchen, the dining room, a smaller formal parlor, and down the hall to the bedrooms. Everything stood in its proper place, some fine pieces here and there, but most of it new and unscarred by time or use. There was little on the walls except occasional prints of famous paintings, bright splashes of color that seemed somehow hollow hanging there.

"You have a very nice home, Melissa," Angie noted truthfully, despite its lack of homeyness.

"It's okay. Papa said we needed to start fresh, you know, when we came up here."

Angie avoided looking into a darkened room to her right, one whose bed was still rumpled. "You don't agree?"

"I guess it's all right. Maybe he needs to do it." She opened the hall's last door and said, "This is my room."

"It's very ..." She stepped inside and finished, "Oh my."

"I asked Daddy and he said it was okay, if it was really what I wanted. And it is. I don't mind Momma's stuff being here. I like it. It makes me remember better."

It had the look of a grown woman's room—the curved dressing table with its hanging pink velvet skirt and mirror top, the big four-poster bed, the grand oval mirror, the two bedside tables, the lamps.

"Daddy doesn't like to come in here much." Melissa went over, and with a little twisting jump she bounced onto the bed. Her legs dangling over the side, she said, "I remember bouncing on the bed on Saturday mornings when I was little. Papa used to growl at me for waking him up, but Momma always giggled. I liked the way she used to laugh."

Angie started a polite response but was halted by the sensation that something important was going on here. Something bigger than what appeared on the surface. "Did your momma sing as beautifully as you and your father do?"

"No, not really. Momma claimed she sounded like a hungry goat. She always said God would need to do a major corrective miracle before He ever let her sing in heaven." She slid from the bed and headed for the double closet. "Momma played the violin. She was very good."

"I'm sure she must have been." Angie watched as Melissa pulled over a chair, climbed up, stood on her tiptoes, and pulled a box off the closet's top shelf. "May I help you with something?"

"No, that's okay." She almost stumbled when descending from the chair, but managed to keep hold of both her balance and the box. She walked over, put it down at Angie's feet, and pulled off the top. "This was Momma's. It's real old."

Angie peered inside and gasped. "Melissa, it's beautiful. May I touch it? I promise I'll be careful."

"All right."

Angie seated herself on the dressing table stool. Melissa stepped back and to one side, as though wanting Angie to shield her from whatever was inside. Angie pressed back the wrapping paper, then lifted up the contents. Melissa told her quietly, "It's a music box."

"I know it is." Angie inspected the small porcelain box with the exquisite figure of a ballerina on the cover, then lifted it up to see the trademark underneath. "Vienna, Austria," she read. "This is simply beautiful, Melissa."

"It plays the song 'Greensleeves,' " Melissa offered quietly.

Something in her tone caused Angie to pause just as she was reaching to lift the top. She turned and saw how the girl was watching, her eyes big and sad. "Would you open this for me?"

Very slowly, Melissa shook her head, back and forth, her eyes not leaving the box.

"Why not, Melissa?"

She did not reply.

"Would you like me to put it back?"

"You can hold it if you want," Melissa replied, her voice as soft as the wind.

"I don't want to make you sad." Hesitantly, Angie reached out and stroked one hand down the side of Melissa's face. The hair beneath her fingers was as fine as silk. "You must have brought this out for a reason. Did you want to tell me something about it?"

A tiny shrug, then a whispered, "When she got sick, Momma listened to this box a lot. She said it reminded her of all the good things, and remembering helped her face what was still to come. That morning, I went in to see Momma, and she asked me to sing. I tried, but I couldn't. I just couldn't. So she asked me to open the box and hold her hand. After a little while, Momma closed her eyes. And she didn't ..."

"Oh, honey." She reached out both arms and enveloped the child. One hand continued to stroke through the soft auburn hair as the other held her close.

They stayed like that for a long time. Then Angie glanced down at the box in her lap and saw how one of Melissa's hands had reached over, and one finger was tracing its way around the delicate figure on the top. The other arm remained wrapped around Angie, as though drawing the strength to reach over and touch the box. And remember.

Angie took a breath and said quietly, "I have a crystal bowl with a cover back at home. A very pretty one. Not as nice as this box, but pretty in its own way. It was the first antique I ever bought. Oh, my mother had some nice things I suppose that's where my interest in antiques comes from. But this was the first one I found for myself. So it has always remained very special to me. It's called a compote jar. Have you ever heard of that?"

A soft voice said, "No."

"Back in the last century, people used to keep a bowl of sweet drink handy for when guests came calling. Sometimes it had spirits in it, sometimes not. And because it was sweet and might attract insects, the bowl had to have a lid on it. In nice houses, the bowl was shaped out of crystal and silver and looked like a plump round vase with a lid."

She did not understand why she was telling Melissa this. But the simple rightness she felt could not be denied. It was not just for Melissa, either. She *knew* this. "After my husband died, I went back to the university and finished learning how to be a teacher. Then I came home. My folks had retired down to the coast, where Daddy got ill and couldn't travel. They left the house here for me. I discovered that it was very hard not to think about my troubles. Even though they had all happened somewhere else, I couldn't just leave them there."

Melissa laid her head against Angie's shoulder. Her arm shifted to the soft space just under Angie's ribs. The quiet voice said, "Neither can Papa. He doesn't say anything, but I know." The auburn head moved back far enough to fasten wide gray eyes upon Angie's face. "And today was the first time I ever heard him talk about, you know, everything."

Angie nodded in understanding and Melissa nodded back. "It made me sad," she explained, "but it was good. I don't know how exactly, but I think it was good Papa talked to you like that."

Angie searched for words but could come up with nothing. She watched the small head nestled back against her and stroked the fine hair. Finally she said, "Where was I?"

"You had problems with your thoughts."

"That's right, I did. And so I decided that something had to change. I couldn't be a good teacher if I was always thinking about the past. But I knew I couldn't keep myself from thinking about those things all the time. I had tried, because I wanted to. But I couldn't. So I decided I could think about whatever I wanted whenever I was home and by myself. But when I went out, I had to leave all those thoughts there at home."

"That must have been hard," Melissa said softly.

"It was at first. But then I put that crystal jar of mine in the front hallway. And every time I left the house, I stopped and saw myself leaving all my inside thoughts there in the bowl. That's what I called them, my 'inside thoughts.' "

She stopped for a moment. She had to. It was only then that she realized the story had an ending. Angie sat there at the dressing table, the music box in her lap and the small form snuggled at her side.

Melissa stirred and without releasing her embrace asked, "What happened next?"

"Well," Angie said with a great sigh, a release of years and years of having nothing *next* to speak of. "One day I discovered that I didn't need the container anymore. And now the bowl has become simply an object of beauty again, not a storehouse for everything that was painful to remember."

Melissa raised her head then. Grave eyes inspected Angie's face, eyes wanting to believe, wanting to be sure that what Angie said was true. "Really?"

"With God, and in God's time," Angie replied. "And now my inside thoughts are just memories. They are sad ones, a lot of them, but still special. I still keep the jar there in the hallway, because I can look at it now and remember, and it's okay."

"It doesn't make you sad?"

"Not anymore," Angie said, meeting the gaze full on. "I feel glad. Glad to be alive, glad to be teaching, glad for all the joy that life still holds for me. It's not perfect, and a lot of things aren't how I would have them be. But I still have a lot to be thankful for."

Big gray eyes continued to regard her. "I wish ..." Then Melissa stopped as she caught sight of something behind them.

Angie turned around to find Carson standing in the doorway. He was leaning against the frame, so still he appeared planted there. His arms were crossed, and he was watching the two of them with an expression that Angie could not identify. His eyes went back and forth from one to the other, then he said quietly, "Lunch is ready."

"Thank you," Angie said, her voice as soft as his.

He turned and walked back down the hallway.

Only then did Angie decide what Carson Nealey's expression had seemed most of all was hopeful.

12

The remainder of the month was spent observing. Angie saw Melissa in class and both of them at church. But other than the occasional smile and brief conversation, there was no contact between them. Angie did not mind. There had been so much contained in that day.

The month's final Friday dawned clear and brilliantly sunny. The temperature was iron-hard cold as she walked to school, but by lunchtime the valley had captured the warmth so that even her sweater felt heavy. As she waited for her last class to gather, she found herself impatiently staring out the window and hoping the weather would hold.

"Miss Picard?"

Angie swung back around. "Hello, Melissa. You caught me daydreaming."

"Yes, ma'am." She held out the folded sheet of art paper. "This is for you."

"Why, thank you." She raised up the paper, read the penciled inscription, "To my friend, Miss Picard. With love, Melissa Nealey." Angie smiled at the girl, anticipation on her face. "This is just too sweet."

"You can open it if you want to," she said shyly.

Angie checked the rapidly filling room. There was little attention cast their way. She knew from experience that the final class before the weekend concentrated mostly on what was to come. She returned to the page in her hand.

The paper had been carefully sealed with a little ribbon. Angie untied the bow, opened the page, and gasped aloud.

"The teacher asked us to draw a picture of spring. I knew this was for you even before I started."

Angie turned so she faced the blackboard and away from the class, all without lifting her gaze from the picture. She swallowed, the sound made loud by the tightness in her throat, the same tightness that turned her voice hoarse as she whispered, "This is beautiful."

"It's the best thing I ever drew," Melissa said simply, standing so she could see both the page and Angie's face. "You like it. I can tell."

"Very much." Angie had to struggle, but she managed a little smile. "I am very touched that you would want me to have this."

"You're my best friend," Melissa replied simply. "I like being able to give you something."

The drawing was mostly pen and ink, done with a minimum of line. It showed a tree trunk, one chopped off a few inches above the ground. The trunk's upper surface was smooth and clean, displaying the whorls and age lines. But that was not what held Angie's attention.

"I got an A for it," Melissa was saying, her voice full of quiet pride. "Miss Jenkins looked at it and got the sniffles."

A single branch had sprouted from the side of the trunk. It rose, slender and fragile, sending out a few tiny shoots of its own. At the top bloomed a single blossom, its pink petals a lone splash of color upon the page.

"It's a cherry tree," Melissa went on. "We had one in our front yard, but it got sick and Papa had to cut it down. Then the spring we left to come here, it started growing that little branch. I've thought about it a lot since we talked. I don't know why."

Angie forced out the pressure in her chest with a long sigh, then folded the sheet, turned in her seat and set it purposefully down on her desk. "I was thinking about taking another trip up into the hills this weekend."

"To buy old things?" The girl's eyes lit up with excitement. "Can I—?" and she stopped, looking embarrassed.

"Yes, please come, if your father says it's all right." Angie patted the folded page once, twice. "Thank you for this gift, Melissa. I'm going to find just the right frame for it. And I will treasure it always."

The highlands at this time of year were great reaches of snowy starkness and lonely roads. Icicles dripped from every branch and rock outcrop. They sparkled like brilliant prisms as the sun marked their passage. Angie drove with determined concentration. The sun meant that the road was clear. But she needed to be back long before the winter-shortened day ended and the water dribbling across the road refroze.

Melissa remained plastered to her window and the front windshield for much of the journey, exclaiming over snowy vistas and half-frozen rivers and vast, empty stretches.

An hour into the drive, however, she announced, "Mrs. Drummond has been talking to me."

"Emma? What about?"

"She wants me to sing a solo for the church this spring."

"Do you want to?"

"I don't know." She kicked absently at the seat. "Sort of."

Angie risked a quick glance. "You're not scared, are you?"

"A little."

"Do you want your father to sing with you?"

Melissa leaned forward, planting both hands upon the dashboard and setting her chin on her knuckles. "I don't want to ask him."

"You don't? Why not?"

"Because he might do it for me," she said, staring out the front. "And he might not be ready to do it for him."

Angie slowed so that she could give the girl a longer glance. "You are very remarkable, Melissa," she said.

Melissa took that as an opportunity to swivel in her seat and ask, "Will you do it with me?"

"Me? I don't ..." Angie stopped herself. A brilliant shaft of sunlight filtered through the trees and transformed the windshield into a sheet of solid gold. As quickly as it came, it disappeared. Angie drove on, searching within, asking herself, *Am I ready?*

With a sudden billowing of excitement, she announced, "I would be delighted to sing with you."

Melissa squeezed her hands together in excitement. The words rushed from her lips. "Mrs. Drummond said if she asked you, you'd say no, but you might do it for me. She said if I asked you and you said yes, she was going to do a jig in front of the whole class."

Angie had to laugh. "You be sure and wait so I can come and see that one for myself."

The rutted lane leading to Mother Cannon's homestead was cleared only as far as the first gate. As they left the car and began trudging through the snow toward the distant cottage, Angie knew this was the only stop they would make that day. Even so, the drive had been a grand success. Despite lingering moments of panic, she was thrilled by the thought of singing again.

Mother Cannon's eldest son came around the side of the house as they drew near. He laid down his ax and basket of kindling and said in greeting, "Got yourself a pretty day for a visit."

"Hello, Clem." Angie stopped at the bottom porch step to kick the snow from her boots and catch her breath. "Have I come at a bad time?"

"No, ma'am. Maw was just saying she'd hope you'd be stopping by. How you been keeping, Miss Picard?"

"Very well, thank you. This is a young friend of mine. Melissa, this is Clem Cannon."

Tall and rawboned, Clem had work-hardened hands sprouting from an ancient but clean shirt. "How do, Missie."

"Hello, sir." Melissa pointed and asked, "Are those suspenders?"

"Yes, ma'am, they surely are." He stuck one thumb behind the elastic and gave it a snap. "Don't they like to keep their pants up, where you're from?"

"They use belts," Melissa replied seriously. "Aren't you cold out here without a coat?"

Clem gave a strong grin. "I got enough work to keep two folks warm."

Mother Cannon pushed through the front door. "It ain't proper to keep guests hanging about in the snow, Clem."

"It's not his fault," Melissa explained for them. "I've never seen suspenders before."

"Is that a fact." Mother Cannon stepped out into the sunlight. "And just who might you be, young lady?"

"Melissa Nealey, ma'am. Miss Picard invited me to come with her."

"Well, if Angie Picard invited you, then, that's good enough for me." She turned back toward the house. "Y'all come on in before you catch your death."

The interior was warm and fragrant with Mother Cannon's baking. Angie let Melissa go first and watched her fascination with everything. She explained to Clem, "She's just moved up from the city."

"Well, I hope she's happy here." Clem was a carpenter whose skills were known throughout the mountain communities, and he could have had enough work to keep him busy ten times over. But he and his quiet country wife loved the hills and the uplands' slower ways, so he took on only what he needed to support his family. He turned to the girl. "You miss the big city and all them lights and noise, Missie?"

"Sometimes." Melissa gave him a quick grin and entered the kitchen. After a slow sweep, she said, "Oooh, this is nice. What smells so good?"

"Been using the last of the cherries I put up to make Clem's brood a few pies." She cast the two adults a smile. "I don't reckon they'd miss a piece or two."

"Long as they don't know about it, and long as

you cut the biggest piece for me," Clem joked, pulling out a pair of chairs, then winking at Melissa. "What brought you up to these parts from the city?"

"My momma died," Melissa said, her tone matter-of-fact. She settled into a chair, unaware of the sudden stillness that gripped the room. "Daddy left his big job and took another one at the shoe company."

Angie cleared her throat. "He's running the factory now."

"You don't say." Mother Cannon came over and took the chair across the table from Melissa. "I'm right sorry to hear about your momma, child. You must miss her."

"I do. A lot." Melissa gave a solemn nod with the words. "But Miss Picard's been teaching me things, and it doesn't hurt so bad anymore."

"Well, I think right highly of Angie Picard."

"Me too." Melissa looked back to where Angie stood alongside Clem. "She's my best friend."

"We all need friends, don't we?" Mother Cannon reached across and took one of the soft young hands with both of hers. "Especially when times get hard."

Clem slipped from the room and returned bearing a hardboard case. "City-bred girl like you, I bet you never heard a country picker before."

"Play us some hymns," Angie encouraged, slipping into the chair beside Melissa.

"Girl's a churchgoer, is she?" Mother Cannon patted the soft hand. "That's good. Real good."

"I stopped going for a while, but Miss Picard has started me back. Papa too." She watched Clem put the strap around his shoulder, run a finger down the strings, then slip the thumb and finger picks into place. "Is this bluegrass?"

"Yes, ma'am, the real thing."

"My momma loved bluegrass."

"Did she, now." He hitched a leg onto a nearby chair. "Then, you can just sing along."

He started with a toe-tapping rendition of "Blessed Assurance." Melissa's auburn hair bobbed up and down in time to the music. Angie exchanged a smile with Mother Cannon, then leaned forward and said quietly, "It's okay, honey. You can sing, if you like."

So she did.

Clem was so startled he lost his place. Mother Cannon settled back in her seat, so as to watch the both of them. Clem glanced at Angie, widening his eyes a trace, and softened his playing to match the girl's voice.

They followed that with "Beulah Land," then "I'll Fly Away." After that, Clem stopped, exchanged a glance with his mother, and asked, "You got any favorites, honey?"

"Momma used to love 'How Great Thou Art.' "

"I believe I can recollect how to play that one." It sounded so good Angie found herself unable to hold back anymore and joined in the singing. Mother Cannon tapped one gnarled hand on the tabletop. Clem swung them back through a second time, then moved directly into "I Surrender All."

When he stopped, the room rang with the fading notes, then silence. Clem slipped off the guitar, walked over and seated himself at the table. He asked his mother, "Did you ever hear the like?"

"A pair of angels have come to tea," Mother Cannon agreed, her eyes on Angie. "Four years I've known you, and this is the first I learn of you having such a voice."

Angie accepted the rebuke with downcast eyes. "I lost it for a while."

"Well, it's a delight to know you've found your treasure again," Mother Cannon said, rising and walking to the oven. "Now, who's going to help me serve this pie?"

They sat and chatted until the shadows began creeping their way along the kitchen cabinets. Reluctantly Angie rose. "We have to be getting back."

"You don't want to risk them high roads at night," Mother Cannon agreed. "Just one second, now, I've got something you might like to take a look at."

While she rummaged in the cupboard, Clem said, "Sure would be nice to have y'all come back and sing with me another time. Got two buddies I'd like you to meet. One picks a mighty mean banjo, and the other can fiddle up a storm."

Melissa turned in her chair, eyes shining. "Can we, Miss Picard?"

"I don't see why not," Angie replied. "Long as

your father doesn't mind."

"Bring him along, why don't you," Mother Cannon said, returning and setting a large parcel upon the table. "He might enjoy a nice country meal."

Angie unwrapped the brown paper. As soon as the item came into view, she exclaimed, "It's perfect!"

"Don't know about that," Mother Cannon replied. "Used to hold a mirror, but one of the young'uns knocked it off the wall."

The oval frame was carved from wild cherry and lined with a second inner frame of hand-beaten copper. "I've been looking for something just like this," Angie said.

"Well, I'm glad you can put it to good use. Now you folks better be getting on the road." As she came around the table, she took hold of Melissa's hand. "Come along here with me, my lady."

Melissa cast a questioning glance back toward Angie but allowed herself to be guided down the hall and through the front door. Angie followed along behind them and watched as Mother Cannon led Melissa to the porch's edge. The old woman slowly bent over so that she could drape one arm across the girl's shoulders. "You see that old maple growing out there in my yard?"

"Sure is big," Melissa said.

"That tree's older than either of us, older than this house, and my daddy's daddy built this place with his own two hands. Look close now, and tell me what you see."

Melissa hesitated, staring out across the snow-covered expanse. "Branches?"

"Looks awful empty, don't it? All them bare limbs, all dark and lonely and cold. You might think that tree is dead, wouldn't you? A sad sight, some folks might say." Mother Cannon shifted slightly, bringing her face up closer so her eyes were level with Melissa's. "But them who know, they understand how times like this are important. More than that, they're *vital*. You know why?"

"No, ma'am," Melissa answered quietly.

"What you're seeing there is only half the tree. You're looking at only what's *visible*. But down underneath the earth, deep where only the good Lord can see, them roots are growing. They're reaching out, gaining hold, anchoring themselves stronger for the spring that's sure to come."

Mother Cannon eased herself upright, looked down at Melissa, and asked, "You hear what I'm telling you?"

Melissa's gaze did not leave the tree. "I think so, yes, ma'am."

"Then, you just reflect on that a time." She stroked the girl's hair a time or two, then added, "And know I'll be keeping you in my prayers."

February became March, carried by a steady flow of beautiful days. That Friday, Angie was clearing her desk, hearing the excited chatter and laughter of youngsters escaping the confines of schedule and school fade into the distance, when there came a quiet knock on her door. Carson stood in the doorway. He wore a well-cut gray suit, a fine silk tie, camel-hair overcoat, and a wool scarf. "I hope I'm not disturbing you."

"No, not at all." Although finding him here, in the center of her little world, was disturbing. "Won't you come in?"

"I heard from Melissa that you like to walk in the afternoons," he said. "I... I was wondering if you might like some company."

Her mind searched for some response but could only settle on, "Melissa has spoken to you about my habits?"

He smiled at that. "My daughter talks about you all the time."

It was his smile and not his words that caught in her heart. She had never seen him smile before, and it transformed his face. All the somber lines lifted at once, gentling the sharp edges. Like a sudden shaft splitting the darkness of an afternoon thunderstorm, the act transfigured him. Angie rose from her chair almost before she realized she had moved. "I'll just get my coat."

Silence accompanied them along the street. The act of walking with a man was so overwhelming in and of itself that Angie felt herself unable to converse. Carson apparently was of the same mind, for he only glanced at her a few times, and that was to share with her another of his smiles. Angie decided that the quiet was not uncomfortable.

Several passing cars slowed to inspect them. Each time, Angie dropped her head, not in shame but rather in confusion. She had never felt quite so on display. It did no good to try to convince herself that she was simply joining the father of a student on her afternoon stroll. She knew what the passersby saw and what they would soon tell all the town. Angie Picard was out walking with a *man*.

For some reason, her chagrin at being the talk of the town was not all that distressing.

It was only when they were approaching her house and she realized she had not opened her mouth a single time since leaving the school that she knew a sudden panic. What if he thought she had not enjoyed the walk? But try as she might, she could not come up with a thing to say, until it occurred to her to ask, "What will you be doing this weekend, Carson?"

He cleared his throat to reply, "I was planning to take my daughter, Melissa, to the cinema tomorrow evening."

As if she needed reminding of who his daughter was. She smiled then, reassured that he clearly felt the same nerves as she. "Why don't you come by first and let me serve you both dinner?"

The next morning, Angie was awake in time to watch the first light of day arrive, clear and cold. She waited as long as she could before picking up the phone and calling Emma's number. "I hope I'm not disturbing you."

"Luke takes it as a personal challenge to beat the roosters," Emma replied glumly. "The day he lets me sleep half as long as I'd like is the day we lay him to rest."

"Do you have your appointment at the beauty parlor this morning?"

"Just like every Saturday. My weekly treat for myself. Why?"

"Do you think you could get them to fit me in?"

Emma was on instant alert. "Angie Picard, you don't mean to tell me the rumors are true."

"What rumors?"

"The ones about you being seen walking bold as day and holding hands with a certain gentleman."

"Emma—"

"I told them it was ripe as last October's pumpkin pie." Emma retreated quickly, but then her voice drew close in the receiver. "It was you, wasn't it?"

"Emma Drummond, do you honestly believe I would allow a man to hold my hand in public? Mercy, I have a reputation to uphold, no thanks to you."

"Well, now, it's got to be something special going on, hand-holding or not. I know on account of you haven't been to a beauty parlor since your momma stopped dragging you down."

"Of all the..." Angie struggled a moment longer, then said weakly, "I don't know why I put up with you."

"Ten o'clock," Emma said with a chuckle. "They'll squeeze you in, or they will have me to deal with. Wait till Luke hears about this one."

When Angie entered the beauty parlor, she was ready for battle. Emma took one look at her face, smiled sweetly, and said, "I've finally decided on the music."

Angie, caught totally off guard, stammered, "What?"

Emma patted the seat beside her. "Come, let her get started."

"Saturdays we don't have a moment to waste, honey," the beautician agreed. "You're lucky we had us a cancellation."

Hesitantly Angie walked over and seated herself. Emma went on, "I've been scouring my books for the right music. I want to give them something they know, but not so familiar they'll try to sing along. I've decided on two English traditionals.

'Alleluia, Sing to Jesus,' by Chatterton Dix, that's one. Then we'll flow directly into 'Under His Wings.' "

Angie realized Emma was talking about the church performance by her and Melissa. She felt the beautician flip back her hair, heard the woman ask, "How you want me to do this, honey?"

"Just a wash and cut, please." She went on to Emma, "You're sure she can learn them in time?"

"She'll do fine, and so will you," Emma assured her, then asked the beautician, "Have you ever heard this lady sing?" She carefully avoided Angie's eyes.

"Never had the honor."

Emma settled back so a second woman could begin washing her own hair. "Angie Picard sounds like I wish I looked."

The hairdresser rinsed and lathered and rinsed Angie with swift, practiced motions. When Angie was back upright, she said, "Nice hair, pretty face, great voice. How come some girls get all the luck?"

Before Angie could think up a response, the beautician working on Emma's hair said, "And still has her figure, ain't that something? You got children, honey?"

Angie shook her head slightly. "No."

"There you are," the beautician said, missing Emma's wince. "That explains it. Ain't nothing that'll put lines on your face and pounds on your middle faster than a couple of young'uns."

"You don't mind my saying, you better get to work on it, " Angie's hairdresser said to her. "You're not a spring chicken anymore, honey."

"Don't you know, that old biological clock just keeps on ticking," the client seated across from Angie agreed. The woman's hair was done up in aluminum foil and frosting dye. Clearly, she found the conversation more interesting than the magazine in her lap.

Another hairdresser announced, "Oh, they're probably just practicing until they get it right."

That drew a big laugh from everybody. Emma tried to cut off the discussion, but her beautician declared, "There's only one thing you need to do when the time comes, and that's *relax*."

"You got that one right," Angie's hairdresser agreed. "You can't get all tensed up about things."

"My best friend," Emma's beautician added, waving her hairbrush for emphasis, "she tried for five solid years, then she adopts, and bam, two months later she's pregnant."

"That happened to my cousin," the woman across from them said. "But you know what else, a friend's sister went to a faith healer, and they laid on hands, and six weeks later she was pregnant with *triplets*."

"Don't get carried away with this children business," Emma's beautician proclaimed. "I've got three teenagers. If you ever want to see why *not* to have kids, come spend an afternoon around my place." She noticed Emma's grim expression. "Is anything the matter, honey?" she wondered.

"I'm late," Emma snapped.

"Don't get yourself in a dither, I'm almost done."

Emma's irritation infected the room, and the remainder of their work was done in silence.

Emma held her tongue until they had paid and left the parlor, but once outside on the sidewalk she spluttered, "I declare—"

"Don't," Angie said quietly. "It doesn't help."

Her friend's big form deflated like a balloon. "I'm so sorry. I had no idea."

"I'd like to say I am used to it," Angie replied. "I suppose in a way I am. But it still hurts."

Emma pulled up short and faced her in astonishment. "Do you know, that is the first time I've ever heard you confess to feeling anything? All this time I've known you, and I've known you longer than anybody in this town, you've never once told me how you feel."

"I'm learning a lot these days," Angie acknowledged. "The lesson of opening up has been a tough one for me, but I'm learning."

"Well, if this doesn't beat all," Emma murmured. She took her friend's elbow and guided her down the street. "You can't imagine the times I have wanted to ask you, to talk with you about it all."

"Why didn't you?"

"Because I've felt like I needed to scale Mount Rushmore before I could get close enough, girl. Why do you think I'm always talking nonsense? It's the only safe conversation with you."

Angie felt the truth hit her with the force of a

hammer. "Emma, I never knew."

"Well, you know now." She glanced over. "So I'm going to ask while I've got the nerve. How on earth do you stand it?"

"With the Lord's help," Angie replied simply. "There is no other way."

They walked along in silence. Angie realized that what she had said was inadequate, that her oldest friend deserved more. She took a breath and plunged in, "I don't ever want to think that tragedy is random—that the fact I couldn't get pregnant, and another could, is just the luck of the draw. That one mother dies, and another child has both her parents until she is old and has children of her own. The temptation to accept randomness as a fact of life is an evil lure. It eats away at all hope."

Emma stopped and fastened sad eyes upon her. Angie went on quietly, "Without faith, I would have had to say, that was just one of those things. It was just chance, a random act of fate. But I could not live with that. I would just shrivel up and blow away. It is faith that keeps me whole. I hope and pray that God will restore the days and weeks and months and years the locusts of pain and disappointment have eaten." She started to turn away.

"Angie, wait." Emma searched her face, as though seeking permission there to express her thoughts. "Did you ever think maybe this new, well, friendship with the Nealeys is a gift to you? One for keeping hold of faith through the hard times?"

"Oh, Emma." The sudden rush of hope and fear

caused Angie to reach out and hug her friend close. "I think I'm happy. But I've been sad for so long, I don't even remember for sure how it feels anymore."

14

Angie found if she thought about the dinner itself, she grew too nervous to accomplish anything at all, much less cook the meal. She rushed through each preparation in order to focus on the next task. Even so, she only completed the final bits just as she heard the car pull up in front of her house.

Melissa came through the gate first, a full twenty paces ahead of her father because of her run up the sidewalk. Watching her progress, seeing the small face beaming behind the bouquet she carried, was enough to wash away Angie's last-minute nerves. She opened the door and smiled back. "What do you have there?"

"Flowers. Daddy said I could carry them, but they're really from both of us." She offered them, shy and proud at the same time. "Aren't they pretty?"

"They're beautiful indeed." Angie stooped to accept them, smelled the gentle perfume, then smiled in Carson's direction.

"Papa told me about your house," Melissa announced. "May I go look inside?"

"Of course you can." She watched the girl hurry around her, then turned and observed the father casting a careful glance over her home. "I really must apologize for the state of my house, Carson. It needs painting and so much else, I wouldn't even know where to start."

"It's a grand place, in its own way. An old house needs constant attention. And you've kept the inside looking nice."

"Yes, that's about all—"

Her words were cut off by a girlish squeal from within. "Papa! Come look!"

Angie smiled and followed Carson inside. The auburn head was now utterly still as Melissa pointed at the oval frame hanging above the side table. "That's my drawing," she breathed. "She hung my drawing in her house!"

Carson stared at the picture for a long moment, then at his daughter. "You drew this?"

"I told you about it, Papa. In art class. Remember the cherry tree you had to chop down?"

He gave a single slow nod. "This is very good, Melissa."

"It is a treasure," Angie said quietly.

"Oooh, doesn't it look nice in that frame?" Melissa hugged herself with pleasure.

"Here, let me take your coats. And thank you so much for the flowers, Carson. You really shouldn't have."

Melissa slipped her arms out of the sleeves without taking her eyes off the picture. Angie ushered them into the dining room, then left the kitchen door open so she could continue talking while she filled the serving dishes.

Melissa made herself at home with cheerful chatter about school, about the summer to come. Carson listened with a quiet intensity, his gaze direct and watchful between Melissa and Angie. She found that she did not mind either his silence or his gaze. Eventually Angie described each of the antiques Melissa could see from her chair, a discussion that took them right through dinner and into dessert. She tried to remember stories attached to them or their purchase. Afterward she listened as Melissa recounted for her father the story of Mother Cannon and Clem and the guitar picking and the songs and the little country house.

Step by step, the food and the atmosphere and the company worked its miracle on Carson. By the time dessert was served, his quiet reserve had dissolved into an occasional comment and an almost-constant smile.

After two helpings of brown sugar pie, Melissa's gaze had become a little owl-eyed. Angie took her upstairs to the spare bedroom and showed her the big hope chest carved from wild cherrywood and polished to a rich rosy luster. She opened the top and was rewarded with a gasp of pure pleasure. "You can take them out, but be very careful."

"They're beautiful," breathed Melissa. "And look, their heads are painted glass!"

"China," Angie corrected. "They are called china dolls. Each one is handmade."

"Oh, look at this one," Melissa said, lifting a

doll in a gown of lace and lavender. "Is she old?"

"Old as Mother Cannon. Some are even older." She watched as Melissa gingerly placed the dolls in a row beside the chest and then rose to her feet. "Put them back and come on downstairs when you're finished."

She returned to the dining room, poured Carson a cup of coffee, and asked if he would be more comfortable in the living room. "I'm settled here," he said. "That was a delicious meal, Angie. Thank you for inviting us over."

"It was a pleasure having you," she replied, wishing the words sounded less formal.

But Carson did not seem to mind. "You've done wonders for Melissa. I was worried about her, I don't mind telling you. She was like a wraith after her mother died."

"Like her father," Angie said, then instantly regretted it. She brought a hand to her lips and said contritely, "I'm so sorry. That was awful."

"But true." Carson turned his chair sideways and stretched out his legs. "And she didn't have a factory to keep her occupied."

"Tell me about your work."

"The place is so old it looks ready to fall down around our ears," Carson said. "Anything more than that would just bore you to tears."

"Nonsense. Nobody living in this town can afford to take such an attitude toward the company."

He gave her a keen look. "That's part of why I'm so interested in it. How important it is to the town."

"Tell me," she urged. "I'd really like to hear."

Haltingly at first, then with increasing focus and energy, Carson described what he had found and what he was trying to do. Angie listened with one ear to his words and the other to how he spoke. She heard a desire to involve himself in the town and its welfare. She heard a man who had become deeply bound to the employees and their families.

And as she listened, she found a gentle stirring within her heart, one so alien it took her a moment to comprehend what it was.

"I want to get us just as ready as I can," Carson was saying, his gaze extended far beyond the confines of her little home. "Sooner or later, the parent company is going to decide we don't fit with their corporate goals. When that happens, I want us to have a strong enough cash reserve to go independent."

She started to ask him to explain what he had just said, but she held back, for she could see how deeply involved he was. There would be time enough for questions later. And the realization gave her heart another quiver.

"This company is in a make-or-break situation for the employees, for their families, and for this town," Carson went on. "It's not right to have so much hanging on a decision taken by a board who have never even been here, much less become involved in this valley. We need to take back control, keep it here among the people who make it work. I'd like to set up a stock-sharing plan, granted to every employee. Give them a chance to be rewarded for the loyalty they've shown."

"I think that is wonderful," Angie said quietly, no longer able to remain silent.

He lifted his head with a start. "Do you really?"

It was Angie's turn to look down at the table, uncertain and nervous. But sure of what she needed to say. "Your daughter has been teaching me a number of lessons."

"Melissa? How?"

"Just by being who she is." Angie took a deep breath. "One thing I have learned from her is how to let go, at least a little. To speak not just my mind, but my heart as well." She raised her gaze and took refuge behind her schoolteacher's tone. "I would like to tell you what I think of your plan."

He responded with a single nod, his reserve again in place.

"I have two reactions. One about what you said and one more personal. About your plans, I have to say that they are not only worthy, they are inspired. I am deeply honored that you would tell me about them, Carson. And I will pray that you are successful beyond your most hopeful dreams."

The tension eased from his shoulders and a deep warmth filled his dark eyes. "And the personal?"

"The personal," she said, the words a sigh. She toyed with her coffee spoon for a moment, no longer able to meet his eyes. "I cannot remember the last time I have spoken about the future. Nor can I recall when I last felt that it might be time to think about dreams of my own."

She forced herself to raise her eyes. "I am deeply grateful that you would give me a reason to look beyond this day, Carson. Very grateful indeed."

He studied her face for a long time, then said, "May I call on you again?"

"I would be so very pleased if you would," she

said, her voice much lower than usual.

Melissa's tread came down the stairs, drawing them back, but not before they had shared a shy smile of discovery. When she came into view, she announced, "We've missed the movie."

"So we have," Carson agreed, glancing at his watch and rising to his feet. "It's time we were going."

"Just one moment," Angie said, rising with him. "There's something I want to show your daughter before you go."

She led Melissa down the front hallway, stopped before the side table, and lowered herself until their faces were level. Melissa glanced at her, then followed Angie's gaze to where it rested upon the ornate crystal compote bowl.

It was shaped somewhat like a broad vase with a lid. The sides were segmented and deeply carved with a floral design. The wider sections were deepest blue. Each floral design was lined with silver filigree.

"That's the one you told me about, isn't it?" Melissa's voice was scarcely above a whisper. "The jar for your inside thoughts."

Angie nodded. "That is the one."

"It's very pretty." She reached out a tentative finger and traced her way down the surface. "What makes this color?"

"It's called cobalt blue. The crystal is melted and mixed with the chemical before it's carved. And the silver is worked in very carefully once the flowers have been formed," Angie replied. "I have no idea where it came from. Isn't that strange? I can't even remember where I found it."

Melissa started to lift the lid, then stopped. She turned and looked at Angie.

Angie nodded a second time, understanding that it was her task, not Melissa's. She hesitated a long moment, inspecting the bowl. The crystal lid was wrapped with a flowering silver vine, which joined at the top to twine about a large silver acorn. Angie grasped the handle and lifted. As the lid came free, it touched the side of the bowl, and the hallway rang with the bell-like chime of crystal upon crystal.

Melissa looked inside. There was another moment's silence, then she said, "It's empty."

"Yes," Angie agreed quietly. "So it is."

That night, after they were gone and the house resounded with the quiet echoes of their departure, Angie opened the living room cupboard and began searching. She knew it was time. Part of her wanted to hold back, while another wanted to go ahead, step forward, accept the challenge. She flipped through her collection of records until she found the one she had been avoiding for months, ever since her first talk with Melissa. She opened the top of the cabinet, turned on the phonograph, and slipped the album from its cover.

She put the music on and felt as though she instantly knew Melissa's mother.

"Scheherazade" was not as most classical music, rising to a single crescendo. The symphony contained far too much passion to run up a steep incline, shout a single cry, then slide into quiet submission. It was a rising series of peaks, like great waves upon a storm-tossed sea, flinging their emotional froth far and wide. Occasionally a flicker of light and calm would flash through, breaking into the tumult with joy and peace, only to be swept up again in the next exultant charge.

Yes, she understood a bit of this woman, this

wife who had left such a hole in two hearts and lives. Angie stood before the phonograph, hugging herself tightly, her eyes closed, swaying in time to the music. She could almost see the woman, not as in a picture, but rather in her heart.

Angie saw someone who would have looked so contained to the outside world, like a proper orchestra in formal wear, all black and white and appropriate. Then there came the moment when the woman's heart would open, and the undeniable truth of her emotions came clear. She released them, letting them run free, unfettered by time or the sweep of common events and ordinary people, unbounded by this world. A rushing river of feelings. Oh yes, Angie could feel the depths of this woman who had shared Rimsky-Korsakov's passion for the unbounded, the almost impossible, the unearthly.

The emotions ran from horizon to horizon. They began long before the music started and soared on afterward into infinity. The music was itself an instrument through which feelings and dreams and passions could emerge, exposing both gifts and destinies. Angie stood and listened, and she felt as though she danced with the woman who was no longer there.

Angie began moving about the room, touching each of her beloved possessions in turn, feeling the need to anchor herself to the here and now. Even so, she sensed a presence. She could not explain it, but she knew there was more at work here than just the music and her imagination.

She sank into a chair and lowered her head to her knees. A single flute rose above the strings and drums, a chanting melody too fragile to contain such emotions. Yet there it was, rising further still, joined now by a single chiming bell, now by a clarinet, now by a violin, now a horn, its lilting melody somehow powerful enough to lead the entire orchestra in a totally new direction.

Angie listened, and then she prayed. The words seemed to come from outside herself, then deep into her heart, finally to soar upward to God. Words praying that she rely not on her own strength, but rather on the strength of God. Words as light as air, yet as powerful as the music's passion. Words of trust, of giving, of healing, of hope.

16

In the weeks that followed, Angie's world became split in three. To the outside world of town and school and church, she showed her usual reserve and proper demeanor. That way she could hold to what she had built for herself, she repeated internally whenever she gave it thought. Just in case things did not work out. She could always return to how things had been before.

Her second world was the one built around Melissa and the joy she saw in the girl continuing to open up, to reach out. They talked together after school. They drove occasionally up into the highlands, just the two of them, watching as winter melted and ran in shimmering rivulets toward spring. They met with Emma to prepare for their duet. Angie felt a special thrill learning the song by Chatterton Dix, especially the second verse, which read:

"Alleluia, not as orphans
Are we left in sorrow now;
Alleluia, He is near us,
Faith believes, nor questions how."

The third world was the one that gave her trouble.

Her time actually spent with Carson ran smoothly, but when she was once again alone, she found fears awaiting her every turn. Memories of her first marriage and the horror of being abandoned woke her up at night, her heart beating so hard she feared it would leap from her chest. She could only rise and pace the room, trying to recall the prayers she had spoken and say them anew. But in the depths of her lonely nights the words seemed like dust, and she felt little comfort, only the chilling prospect of being hurt once again.

So she became distant to Carson. It was she who set the tone of their walks and their dinners and their drives down to the city for a concert or shopping or simply an excursion on their own. He responded with his quiet reserve. She was sure that he was uncertain about what she was feeling or how he should act. Yet she could tell that he was growing increasingly close to her, and that frightened her even more.

They had taken to walking together in the evenings, a time that she treasured more than she wanted to admit even to herself. Most evenings, the silence between them was comfortable, and Angie found herself relaxing, reaching out, happy to be there, wanting the moment to last forever.

Yet when they started up the front walk to her house, and she looked up at the home's sad and peeling exterior, Angie felt as though she was confronted by an image of herself. There in the deteriorating house did she see how the past and the pain had aged her.

At that point, all her current feelings became pressed together with everything that had come before, and the tumult turned her cool and distant. And after he departed, her fears rose like thunderclouds, and her thoughts speared her like sudden bolts of lightning.

Even so, Carson kept coming and walking with her. He seemed willing to allow things to continue as they were for as long as necessary.

But they could not. In her nervous nightly pacings, Angie knew that if she were to go on as she did now, something would happen. Something would come and shatter what was being built.

Her musings troubled her such that Carson could not help but notice. The first Monday of April, he finally interrupted her internal struggle by asking, "Is something troubling you, Angie?"

Not even his concerned tone could ease Angie's sense of suddenly being pressured. "Why would you ask such a thing?"

"Your brow's been furrowed all evening." He paused to cough. He had been troubled by a wracking wheeze for several days now, but insisted it was just a cold he couldn't shift. He recovered and went on, "You look as worried as I've ever seen you."

Angie sighed. She had never in her life felt so torn in two. "I'm just a little concerned about some things."

"Would you care to talk about them?"

She walked on a moment, struggling with all she felt. The first buds of spring were beginning to appear. Gardens sprouted tulips and slender crocus shoots. The willows and the cherry trees looked brushed with strokes of golden-green. She scarcely saw any of it. "I... I don't think I can. But thank you for asking."

Carson reached over and took her hand. It shocked her, both the act itself, and how comfortably it fit to the moment and to her. He said softly, "I've been learning from you how important it is to share things, even when it's difficult."

But it was all too much, the pressures from within and without, the fears and the night terrors and the memories and the future. She drew her hand away. "Carson—"

"It would be nice to offer that gift back to you," he went on. Carson coughed again, almost doubling him over. He straightened, his cheeks flushed from the effort, and gave a shamefaced smile. "I'm sorry. That was not a very inviting way to share confidences."

"I don't think ..." She was going to say that she did not think she could allow their relationship to continue. But she was forced to stop in mid-sentence. Much as she wanted to end the walk and the talk and their time together, much as she desired to halt all the confusion and turmoil right then and there, she could not. The words simply did not come. They were cut off tightly, as though a giant hand had taken hold of her throat and was squeezing it shut.

"Try," he urged softly, misunderstanding her struggle. He stopped to face her, his breath coming in a rattling wheeze. "You've been so tense lately, I've been sure you had something troubling you. Please let me help, Angie." His gaze held heartfelt concern.

"I can't—" Once again the words were cut off. Not stopped by her own will, but rather simply closed away. As though all the prayers and searchings of all her lonely nights were crowding in there, keeping her from halting the flow of time and events that had been set in place for her. For *her*.

And in that moment of indecision, there came again the resounding message, the silent words, *Share Yourself*. The way was left open, to speak, to tell him of her troubles and fears. The invitation being offered was clearly something beyond Carson's gentle encouragement.

But Angie dropped her head in defeat and whispered only, "I can't."

"Well, perhaps another time," Carson said, obviously disappointed.

They walked on, the silence broken sporadically by Carson's coughing. When they arrived at her front walk, he halted and said, "I'll bid you good evening, then."

With the force of a gust of winter wind across her face, Angie felt a solid knowledge that she was walking away from something vital. Something that might not come again. She opened her mouth to speak, to pour out her heart, but the tumult and the fear held her back.

Perhaps inside, she thought. Perhaps there she would be able to tell him. "Won't you come in?"

"Not tonight," he said, and the folds of his young-old face creased in tight concern. "Melissa came home with another cold. I need to get back and see how she's doing."

"Of course," she said. She watched him turn away and felt new defeat wash over her.

The following week, Angie stood by the classroom window as Thursday's final class straggled in. A saffron veil hung over the valley. The afternoon sun had just touched the high peak west of her, and the rays tinted the gently billowing mist the color of a lily. Angie scarcely saw it at all.

Since their talk, Carson had not come by. Each evening she had waited until darkness threatened to make any walk impossible, then started off alone. These solitary outings had become times of remorse and regret. A half-dozen times each evening she would reach for the phone, only to turn away, knowing she would be unable to say what she should, frightened by the prospect of hearing that he had grown impatient with her coldness and reserve.

What was more, Melissa had not been in class at all that week.

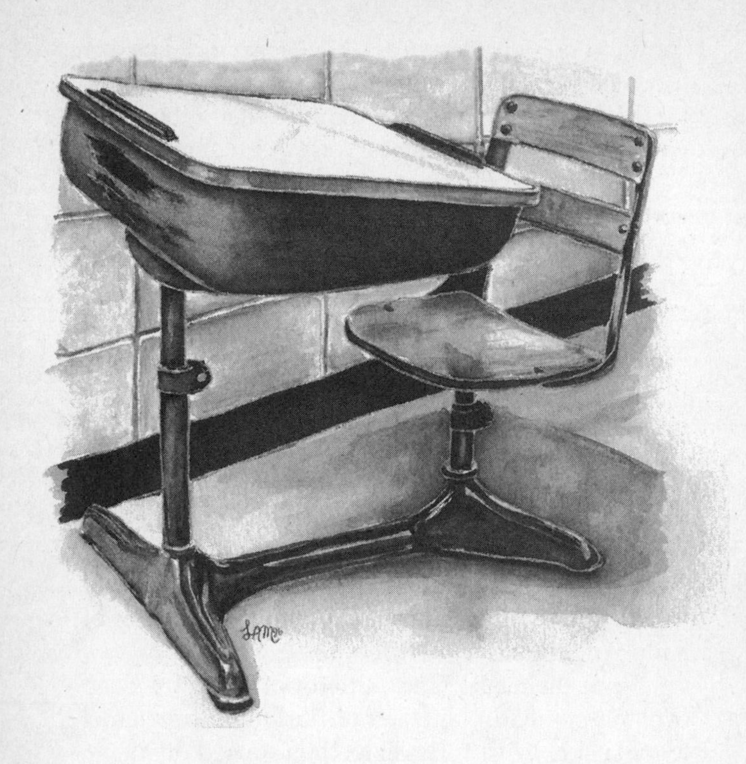

When the bell sounded, she turned back to the class and felt a solid chill spread through her at the sight of Melissa's desk, empty once again. The worry and the dread solidified into certainty.

"Get out your textbooks, turn to the end of chapter sixteen."

The urgent edge to her tone brought a swift and silent response. Angie went on, "I want you to answer all the questions listed on the chapter's final

page. Take your time. You may reread the pages if you need. If I am not back by the end of class, leave your papers on my desk. This will take the place of next week's test, so do your best here."

Astonished glances were exchanged around the class. But Angie did not have time to explain. "Mr. Whitley, bring your book and papers and come up here, please."

The biggest youth in the class, a traditional mischief-maker saved from being a real problem by a good heart and a fine sense of humor, gave a worried look about him as he did as he was told.

"Sit here at my desk," she ordered, and while he recovered from the shock, she cleared a space for him. Once he was seated, she leaned over and spoke with all the urgency she could muster. "I need your help. Can I count on you to make sure that the class maintains both silence and decorum?"

"Sure, Miss Picard," he stammered and seemed to expand at the sudden gift of responsibility.

"Thank you." She straightened. "Remember, treat this as a test." Then she left.

The principal was not in his office. Angie frantically scouted the halls, wondering whom she could disturb. Then Emma came down the side stairwell, her arms full of music scores. Angie rushed over. "Did you drive in today?"

"Of course. Angie, honey, what's the matter?"

"Can you take me up to the Nealeys?" Already she was urging the larger woman through the doors and down the stairs and toward the parking lot. Her

words tumbled over each other. "I need to get over there right now. I didn't bring my car—"

"Is something the matter with Melissa?"

Angie waited until they were in the car and starting down the drive to respond. "She hasn't been in for six days, no, it's seven, and Carson said she had a cold. Oh, I don't know, I don't know, I'm very worried."

"Look at you. I've never seen you in such a state."

Angie leaned forward in her seat, urging the car to greater speed. "I've had a feeling all day that something is wrong."

"You sound just like a mother," Emma said, then a hand flew to her mouth. But Angie barely heard her.

When they pulled up in front of the Nealey home, Angie had her door open before the car rolled to a halt. She spotted Doctor Thatcher coming out of the front door and rushed over. "How are they?"

"I was hoping you were the ambulance." Thatcher was old and graying and recently had brought in a young man to gradually take over his practice. But the town still revered the old man and where possible sought him out. Today he looked tired and strained. "They should have been here by now."

Angie gripped her chest with one hand. "Is it Melissa?"

"It's both of them, and that's the problem. Bronchitis, hopefully not pneumonia, but at this stage it's hard to tell for certain." He snapped his

black bag shut. "Carson's been trying to take care of her by himself, and he's got a fever hot enough to keep him flat on his back. The girl would probably be better off staying here, but she needs watching. I don't like the sound of that chest."

Doc Thatcher glanced behind him. "I've had the dickens of a time getting Carson to let me take her. And the little girl's in there crying her eyes out, which won't help her congestion one bit. She doesn't want to leave her daddy."

"Call the ambulance," Angie said in the same tone she used on her class. "Tell them not to come."

"Angie Picard, what are you talking about? I'm telling you, that child needs round-the-clock watching, and the father is in no state—"

Cutting off further argument, she walked back to where Emma stood uncertainly. "Can you go by my house and pick up some things?"

"What's the matter?"

"I'm going to need to stay here and help out for a while." She scrambled through her purse, came up with a marking pencil and an old envelope. "Both of them are down with chest colds. He wants to send Melissa off to the hospital."

"Angie, if Doc Thatcher thinks—"

"She needs looking after, and she needs her home," Angie said, thrusting the envelope and her keys into Emma's hands. "Doc Thatcher can look in on her from time to time, and if things get worse ..." She stopped, then said, "Just come back whenever you can."

Emma started to argue further, saw the set of Angie's chin, and changed tacks. "I'll stop by the grocers for some things. Never seen a bachelor's pantry that didn't need restocking."

"Fresh vegetables and a good chicken," Angie said. "I'll make up a big batch of chicken soup. Never seen a sickness yet that didn't respond to country penicillin."

17

The crisis struck on the third night.

Doc Thatcher had left a few hours earlier. He stopped in every morning and evening; he first checked on Carson, then listened to the girl's chest and measured her temperature, then listened again. Angie always sat beside him, helping Melissa to sit up so he could place the stethoscope on her back.

After his last inspection, he had taken Angie into the hallway and said quietly, "She might need the hospital, Angie."

"She'd hate it worse than anything."

"I know. But her chest is congested, and I can't seem to shift that fever. Putting her under an oxygen tent might give her some help breathing."

She started to protest, then saw the genuine concern in his eyes, and stifled her own fears. "Do what you think best."

He pursed his lips, studied the floor at his feet, and decided, "We'll give it one more day. If it's no better tomorrow evening, I'll have to move her over to Parker Memorial."

"I'll have her ready," Angie promised. "How is Carson?"

"Improving. He's older and stronger and got a

powerful will, that fellow. He'll be fine, now that somebody's here to see he stays in bed and rests." Doc Thatcher fastened her with a keen eye. "What about you?"

"Me? I'm fine."

"You don't look fine. You look just about done in. Are you sleeping any?"

"Now and then. I get enough rest."

"See that you do. You won't be helping anybody, wearing yourself out so you wind up flat on your back." He patted her shoulder and headed down the hall. "You have my number in case anything changes."

"Right beside the phone."

Ten minutes after he left, Emma pulled up. When Angie answered the doorbell, Emma took one look at her friend and said, "You look like a used washrag. When was the last time you lay down?"

"I'm fine," Angie said flatly and changed the subject. "What's that you've got there?"

Emma hefted the casserole dish. "Shepherd's pie. I thought Carson might be ready for some stick-to-his-ribs food."

"Umm, it looks good. I might have some too. You're a dear," Angie said, taking the dish.

"And you are a saint." Emma glanced into the house. "How are they?"

"Carson is improving. Doc Thatcher's worried about Melissa. He may move her to the hospital tomorrow."

"Poor little thing." Emma searched her purse

and came up with a pair of get-well cards. "One of these is for Melissa. All my classes signed it for her. The other one's for you."

Angie set the casserole down on the side table. "For me?"

"I was worried about people talking—you know, you being here alone and all. But I was wrong, what I said about people talking. They're talking, all right, but it's all good. Carson's made himself some friends around the factory and the town. Folks are glad he's got somebody like you seeing after him and the child."

She handed over the cards. "Friends from church all signed this for you. I'm off to Bible study now. We'll be praying for you as well as them in there."

Angie repressed a sudden shudder. "Give everyone my thanks."

"I will." Emma searched her face. "What's the matter?"

"Oh, nothing." But there was no place here for hiding things. Nor need. "I just had this sudden memory of a prayer group I was with down in the city. The week before the doctors gave me the final news that I couldn't have children, they prayed over me. One of the ladies looked up and said, 'I see you holding a baby born in June.' "

"Oh, honey," Emma sighed.

"I wanted so to believe it," Angie said, and suddenly felt her strength leave her. She leaned against the doorjamb and went on, "Then my husband left, and June came and went, and all I had was a hole in my heart. Were they wrong? Was God wrong? Was I not a proper believer? The questions were so painful I tried not to think for the longest time."

"The things you've been through," Emma murmured.

"That summer, I stayed as busy as I could with summer courses, anything to keep my mind occupied. But it seemed like every time I went out I was seeing babies everywhere. Every other person in the supermarket was a mother with a stroller. Every other person in church was part of a family."

Emma reached out and enveloped her friend. "You are part of a family, honey. *Our* family. I love you like you were my own sister." She released Angie and wiped her cheeks. "Now I want you to promise you'll call me if there's anything you need."

Angie thanked her and hugged her a second time, then waved her down the walk. It was only when she shut the door that she heard a weak call from the other end of the house.

Angie flew down the hall, saw that Carson had not wakened, and raced into the back bedroom. "What's the matter, honey?"

The flushed little face looked at her, the eyes terror stricken. "I thought you had left and gone away forever."

"Shhh, sweetheart, it's all right. It was just a fever dream." Angie reached for the bowl of ice and water, dipped in the cloth, and wiped Melissa's face. She looked so tiny in that giant bed.

"Everything is going to be fine."

"Just like Momma." A hot hand gripped her own with surprising strength. "Promise me you won't go away and leave me alone."

"I'll be right here," Angie soothed, but her heart had become so full that the words were a little hoarse. "You try to rest now."

"I woke up and you weren't here and I got so scared," Melissa said.

"I'm not going anywhere; don't you worry."

She was silent for a long moment, comforted by the cloth and by Angie's touch. Then she started to rise. Angie pressed her back, saying, "Stay still, Melissa. What do you need? I'll get it for you."

"The box," she whispered, looking toward her closet.

"Your music box?" Angie hesitated. "You want me to bring it here?"

Melissa nodded, her feverish gaze on the closet door.

Angie wavered a moment, then walked over, reached to the top shelf, and brought down the box. She carried it back to the bed. "Do you want me to set it here on the table?"

"Let me do it," Melissa said, reaching over. With difficulty she turned the gilded key, hesitated a long moment, then lifted the lid with the ballerina seated on it. The silvery tones of "Greensleeves" filled the room.

Melissa lay on her side, listening to the music. A single tear welled up and traced its way down her cheek.

Angie started to close the lid, but before she could move, Melissa whispered, "Leave it open, please. Will you hold me?"

"Oh, my dear, of course I will." Angie set the box on the side table, moved the bowl, and stretched out beside Melissa. She felt hands reach over and curl up under her chin as the small body pressed close. From the table, the music chimed along in brilliant cadence.

Angie found herself remembering an early Christmas, when she had sung her first church solo. The song had been "What Child Is This," sung to this very melody. She held the little body close. Strange that she would think of such a thing now.

And then Angie heard, soft as a whisper, Melissa sing, "This, this, is Christ the King, whom shepherds guard…" But the voice drifted to a stop as she caught her breath. Angie squeezed her tightly.

"I wish Momma could have met you," Melissa whispered, snuggling even closer. "She would have loved you. I just know it."

Angie searched for something to say, but could only lie and stroke the silken hair. Then a thought occurred to her. She looked down at the little auburn head and asked, "When were you born? I don't think I know your birthday."

"The first of June," came the whispered reply as Melissa drifted ever closer to sleep. "Momma always called my birthday the herald of summer."

June.

18

Angie awoke to sunshine and birdsong and a small form still tucked up against her. She raised her head and discovered that Carson was standing in the doorway, robe wrapped up close to his chin, his eyes fastened upon the pair of them. As quietly as she could, Angie eased her arm out from beneath Melissa's head. The child stirred but did not awaken. She slid from the bed, walked over, studied his face, and whispered, "You're feeling better."

He nodded. "So is Melissa."

Angie turned back to the bed and felt an enormous flood of relief when she saw that it was so. The fever-flush was gone, replaced by the pale shadow of weakness. In that instant Angie knew for certain that recovery had begun.

"I've made coffee," Carson whispered. "Come join me when you're ready."

When Angie entered the kitchen, Carson filled a cup and put it down in front of her, then seated himself across from her. "I can't thank you enough for everything you've done. I don't know how we would have managed on our own."

His gaze was gentle and deep, filled with a peace that Angie felt disarm every one of her barriers.

Carson went on, "I've watched you these past few days and seen how you care, and I've felt so reassured."

"Reassured?" Angie set down her cup. "Why?"

"You've been so distant the past few weeks," he said slowly. "I was afraid I'd done something to drive you away."

"Carson—"

"No, wait, let me finish. I've never been good at talking about my emotions, and even worse since, well, for the past three years. You've taught me so much, and shared so much, and when I felt you drawing away from me ..." He hesitated a moment, then lowered his eyes and finished, "I felt as though I had lost you. And it hurt worse than I could bear."

"Carson, I've been such an idiot." She reached across and took his hand. "You didn't do anything wrong. It was me. I've been so frightened, and for all the wrong reasons."

He raised his gaze. "Then, you weren't angry with me?"

"Oh no. Not at all." She felt his other hand across her own, the warmth and comfort coursing through his touch, easing away her reserve. "I was hurt so terribly. I never thought I'd ever, well ..."

"Love again," he murmured softly.

She nodded, feeling the heat in her chest and the burning in her eyes, and whispered, "Yes."

"Neither did I. And when it came, I couldn't believe it. Didn't want to believe it. But it's true." He searched her face. "I know it's a lot to ask, coming into your life with a child who's not yours. But I love you so, I've lain there in my bed and known this as clearly as anything I've ever known in my entire life. Do you think you could ever love me—love us?"

"I do," she whispered. "I do so already."

The grip on her hands strengthened. He waited until she had raised her gaze to meet his own, then asked, "Angie Picard, would you marry me?"

"Oh, Papa ..." The soft voice from the kitchen doorway drew their startled glances, then all three were laughing and crying and hugging.

19

Even though she had been ready and waiting for almost two hours, still the doorbell seemed directly connected to her head and jangled every nerve in her body when it sounded. She hurried down the front hall, opened the door to a beaming young face. "I declare, I thought you'd never get here."

"Don't you start," Emma called from the car. "We're ten minutes early."

"Never mind. Oh, now where did I put my purse."

"It's right here," Melissa said, picking it off the doorknob, then turning and calling back to the car, "You were right, Miss Emma. She's nervous."

"I am not either," Angie restarted, rattling the keys as she struggled to lock the door. "And I'd have every reason to be if I were."

Melissa hurried down the walk beside her. "Miss Emma says we're gonna knock them dead."

"What an appropriately delightful way to describe a duet for a Sunday worship," Angie said, climbing into the car.

"Good morning to you, too," Emma said, putting the car in gear.

"I can't believe I let you talk me into riding to church. I probably won't have any composure at all without my morning walk."

"You can loosen your grip on that purse, dear," Emma said. "That is, unless you aim on tearing it in two."

Angie's rejoinder was cut off by the sight of a familiar truck driving by. Hammond Whitley, Mark Whitley's father, was the town's finest builder. But this morning, the truck seemed to coast by the ladies on its own. The crest of a paint-spattered hat was all that could be seen of the driver, as though he had slumped down below the wheel. "Was that Ham?" Angie asked.

"It couldn't be," Emma said, shoving her foot down on the gas pedal. "And if it was, I'll shoot him myself."

Melissa giggled from the backseat. Emma glared at her in the rearview mirror. "I'll thank you to keep hold of whatever it is that's tickling you, young lady."

Angie peered at her friend through squinted eyes. "Emma Drummond, what mischief have you got cooking?"

"Me? Huh. As if I had enough time for anything, what with three teenagers, four classes, Luke's hardware store, and a pair of singers so nervous they'd fly out the window if I didn't keep it rolled up tight."

"I'm not nervous, and you're avoiding my question."

"If I told you once I've told you a thousand times, you're worse than my youngest for dreaming up nonsense."

"Speaking of your children," Angie queried suspiciously, "why aren't they with you this morning?"

"Oh, they're with Luke." Something about the question left Emma flustered. She picked up her program from the seat between them and began fanning herself. "I declare, it's more like July than late April."

The road wound into town, a series of curves made graceful by the bounty of cherry trees blooming on either side. The blossoms were at their height that weekend, each tree bursting with white and pink. The gentle fragrance lingered on the tongue, sweet as honey, light as air. "Where is Luke?"

"In his truck," Emma said, her agitation increasing as Melissa stifled another tiny giggle. "Now, why don't you think about what's just up ahead. Do you have your music?"

Angie proceeded to make a frantic search of the seat around her. "Oh my goodness, wait, you'll have to turn around."

"It's right here, Miss Emma," Melissa sang out from the backseat. "I picked it up from her hall table."

"Bless you, child. It's good to know somebody's able to keep hold of their wits this morning." Emma heaved a sigh of genuine relief when they rounded the corner and the church came into view. "Now, come on, let's go greet the folks."

There seemed to be a determined effort by everyone at church to share a smile and half a secret with her. Their gladness was infectious, even with Angie, even on that particular Sunday.

Then the crowd parted, and there before her stood Gina. A smiling, happy woman, dark-haired and vibrant, inspecting her with those piercing black eyes, then lifting her arms and walking forward and hugging Angie close. To her ears alone she said, "You've changed, my dear. Oh, how you've changed!"

All Angie could manage was, "What? ... How?"

"Miss Gina's been talking with Miss Emma," piped up a very breathless Melissa. "And then Miss Gina called me!"

At Angie's questioning look, Gina said, "I remembered Emma from your wedding. Anyway, I wouldn't have missed this performance for the world." She released Angie long enough to reach into her purse. "I found another passage and wrote it down. Only this one is not for you. It's for all the other people you're going to be able to help." She handed over the card and finished with joyful assurance, "Now that you have found the answer for yourself."

Angie accepted the card and read the neatly printed passage from Isaiah: "In all their affliction he was afflicted, and the angel of his presence saved them: in his love and in his pity he redeemed them: and he bare them up, and carried them."

"This is beautiful," Angie said slowly. She

stared into the smiling face and said, "I can't believe you came all this way just to hear me sing."

Gina looked startled. "Why, don't—"

"Miss Emma's waving at us," Melissa broke in, suddenly frantic. "We have to go right now!"

Angie gave Gina a final hug and then allowed the little form to pull her from the gathering. Emma shooed them around to the tiny changing room used by the choir. "You two get into your robes and go over your songs one more time. I'm going to check on the folks up here."

"Emma—"

"Go on now, anything you've got to say can wait until afterward."

Angie watched the girl slip her robe over her head and begin singing through the first tune. Melissa swayed so her robe flowed out in golden ripples. Angie stood by the wall and watched her dance in little happy circles. Melissa's joy was infectious.

Suddenly Angie was caught by the need to ask something that had been on her mind all week. The thought left her so unsettled she had to sit down.

"Melissa," she started, then caught herself, uncertain how to continue.

"It's okay, Miss Picard," Melissa assured her. "Everything is going to be just fine. Miss Emma says once we start singing, the nerves will go away."

"For once, I think she's probably right." Angie tried to still her flutters, then patted the seat next to her. "Come sit beside me for a moment, please."

When Melissa had settled, Angie hesitated a

moment longer, then said, "It would be nice if you would call me Angie when we're alone like this. That is, if you want."

Melissa beamed. "I'd like that very much. Is that what you wanted to ask me?"

"No." Nervously she clasped her hands in her lap. "Your father and I have been talking about, well, plans for after we're..."

"Married," she said for Angie, almost singing the word. The slim shoulders rose in delight. "Isn't it wonderful?"

"Yes." Angie clenched her hands together and asked, "I was wondering, well, I needed to ask ... how you might feel about perhaps your father and you moving into my house after the wedding. I know it's old and there's more bare wood than paint, but it's been such an important part of my life, I'd really love to make it part of yours as well."

Melissa smiled. "Okay."

"You can have all your things in your own room..." Angie plunged ahead before Melissa's response sank in. "You don't mind?"

"I always thought that's what we would do," she said simply. "I love your house, Miss, I mean, Angie. I think it's beautiful."

Angie leaned back weakly. "You don't mind that it looks a little shabby?"

For some reason, the question caused another giggle to bubble up from inside. Melissa managed to stop it by clamping both hands over her mouth. When she was sure it was past, she let go long enough to ask, "Which room is going to be mine?" Her eyes were gleaming. "Can I have the one with the turret?"

"It's called a gable," Angie corrected. "Of course you can, if that's what you want."

"I do. I think it's a beautiful room, with the windows around the corner like that. Can we keep the chest with the dolls in there? I'll be careful with them."

Angie reached over and took her hand. "They're yours."

"Really?" Melissa's eyes held her delight.

"They're my gift to you. My welcome-home gift."

"Oh, Angie." Melissa wrapped her arms tightly around Angie's shoulders. "That's the best new-home present anybody ever got." Then she released Angie, leaned back, and said, "But can I ask for something else?"

"Of course."

It was Melissa's turn to be nervous. "I was just wondering," she started, then hesitated before ending in a rush, "can you and Daddy get married on my birthday?"

Angie felt the world tilt on its axis.

"Please, please, it would be the best birthday anybody ever had." She rose to stand in front of Angie, their fingers now intertwined. "I already asked Papa, and he said he'd think about it, but I know he was just waiting to get up the nerve to talk with you about it. Please, say it's okay."

"Melissa, sweetheart..." Angie stopped to bite down hard on her lip. Then she said, "That is positively the nicest thing anybody has ever asked me."

"Then, you'll do it?" Her hands were already clapping.

"Of course I will."

She squealed and grabbed Angie for a whirl around the floor. "Oh, this is great! Wait till Papa hears."

Emma chose that moment to open the door. "What is all this racket? People are coming for worship out here." She took one look at Angie and scowled fiercely. "Why aren't you in your robe? We're ready!"

Angie slipped into her robe in no time flat, although nothing could have stopped her from smiling. Nor Melissa. The two of them entered the sanctuary and took their places beside the organist, beaming out at the congregation, waiting for Emma to give them the downbeat.

Angie was so full of the day and the days to come that she scarcely knew she was singing at all. It was only when she was well into the final piece that the music and the moment came into focus. She heard herself blend in perfect harmony with Melissa, and sing,

"Under His wings I am safely abiding,
Though the night deepens and tempests are wild;
Still I can trust Him—I know He will keep me,
He has redeemed me and I am His child!"

20

She would never have admitted it, not even to herself, but Angie was a trifle disappointed with the scant number of comments she and Melissa received after the service. It seemed as though almost everyone was in a hurry to be somewhere else. Even Melissa. She hugged Angie swiftly and said, "That was great, Angie. Bye. I have to go with Daddy."

Angie could only gape and say, "Now?"

"Yes, ma'am. Is it okay if I move one thing into the house today?" The smile filled her whole face. "Just one thing. But I want to go ahead and start."

"I suppose so," Angie said, feeling as though events were coming from the most unexpected directions today. "But what's the—"

Emma bounded into the choir room. "Aren't you ready to go yet? Come on, get out of that robe!"

"Emma Drummond, won't you even say we sang well?"

"All right, all right, you sang well." She shooed Melissa out the door, who turned and gave Angie a little wave before vanishing. Emma went on impatiently, "Hurry up now, time's a wasting."

Angie pulled off her robe. "Well, I never—"

"Come on, come on," Emma urged her out the church's back entrance and around to where the car was waiting. Angie searched the churchyard, but Gina was nowhere to be seen. She allowed herself to be guided into the car, settled herself, and grimly crossed her arms.

When the road curved sharp enough for Angie to see a procession of cars behind them, she turned and saw that Emma was grinning broadly, and declared, "You've got something up your sleeve. Don't you dare deny it."

And then they came up the final rise, and there was her little house. Or was it?

Trestle tables had been set up across her front yard, and women were laying out plates and glasses and knives and forks. Behind them, men were setting up a scaffold under the careful eye of Ham Whitley. Already her entire first floor bore a skirting of pipe and planks.

Angie turned to her friend as they pulled up, too astonished to even ask. Then Luke was at her window, formal now in his shy pleasure, opening the door and offering her a hand. She did not have the strength to either resist or protest. Angie alighted and steadied herself on the car.

"Miss Angie—" Luke began and stuttered to a stop as more and more cars halted and the people piled out, and those in the front yard came down to join them. The crowd grew and grew around them, and all Angie could do was look out over the smiling faces. Years of students there with parents and friends, and friends of her own parents, three and even four generations of the townsfolk standing there and smiling.

"Miss Angie," Luke started anew, only this time a young voice cried, "Wait, wait, we've got to be there too!" A way was made for Melissa and Carson Nealey to move up to the front.

"And me!" The dark hair and a brilliant smile marked Gina's arrival. Her eyes glistened with joy as she beamed at Angie.

Luke's big hands kept turning his hat brim round and round nervously. "Miss Angie ..."

"You said that already, Luke, dear," Emma sang out from the car's other side. "You can skip on to the next part."

"We've noticed your house has been in need of a new coat of paint," Luke said. "And, well, that is—"

"I declare, Luke, there's food getting cold." Emma shouldered her way around to stand in front of Angie. "Honey, you are a friend to everyone in this town, and we all just want to say thank you."

Angie stammered, "For what?"

"For everything," called a voice from the back.

"You've been through a hard time, years more than anybody nice as you deserves," Emma said. A chance ray of sunlight slipped between the wind-rushed clouds and played across the gathering, pausing long enough on Angie to make it hard for her to see clearly. Emma went on, "We just want to celebrate with you now that happiness has come back home."

"And we're gonna paint your house," Luke finished determinedly.

She could not reply. People close up saw the raw emotion on her features and started up the walk. Others took their place, as though everybody needed to glance and see what she was feeling. Just a glimpse, mind. It was enough.

"Don't tell me you aim to stand down here and watch." Emma shook her head, her grin as bright as the sun. "I do wish you could see your face right now."

"Come on, dearest," Carson said, taking her hand. "Let's go say hello to everybody."

Angie let herself be led across the lawn, stopping for hugs here and there, shared words she neither heard nor fully realized she was speaking. Then the music started, and she looked over and saw with a start that Clem Cannon was picking a tune with two other men she knew vaguely from her highland travels. One plucked the strings of a banjo, the other sawed at a fiddle. Mother Cannon looked up from where she was cutting pies and joined in the shared smile.

Clem waved and asked, "Hope you aim on joining us for a song or two, Miss Angie."

"I told Miss Emma," a voice to her side said as a small hand joined hers. "Miss Emma talked to Pastor Rob. Then he talked to me. Then he talked to his momma. And she talked to Clem." Melissa paused long enough to draw breath, then demanded, "Will you come inside with me now?"

Only then did Angie realize that Melissa was carrying the music box. "What are you doing with that, honey?"

"I told you, I wanted to move it into your house today."

"Our house," Angie corrected quietly.

"That's right. *Our* house. Can we go now?"

Angie followed her across the yard and through the front door. The banging and clattering was muffled when she closed the door behind them. Angie asked, "Where shall we put it?"

Melissa shifted the box so that she could point with one hand and say, "Right here, on the table by the door."

A cloud of unseen weight seemed to lift from her heart. "Perfect," she said quietly. "I'll move this bowl of mine upstairs."

"No," Melissa said quickly, putting her box down and opening the lid. As "Greensleeves" filled the hallway, she went on, "Beside your crystal jar. Together. And whenever we come in or go out, we'll look at them and remember the good things."

"That's right," Angie agreed, taking Melissa's hand. "Only the good things."